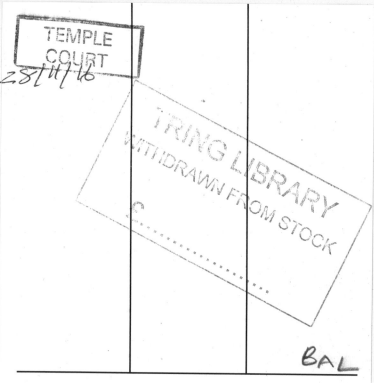

TEMPLE
COURT

28/11/16

TRING LIBRARY
WITHDRAWN FROM STOCK

£ ....

BAL

Please renew or return items by the date
shown on your receipt

www.hertsdirect.org/libraries

Renewals and enquiries: 0300 123 4049

Textphone for hearing or   0300 123 4041
speech impaired user

L32

D1363039

46 402 140 2

SPECIAL MESSAGE TO READERS

THE ULVERSCROFT FOUNDATION
(registered UK charity number 264873)

was established in 1972 to provide funds for
research, diagnosis and treatment of eye diseases.
Examples of major projects funded by
the Ulverscroft Foundation are:-

- The Children's Eye Unit at Moorfields Eye
  Hospital, London
- The Ulverscroft Children's Eye Unit at Great
  Ormond Street Hospital for Sick Children
- Funding research into eye diseases and
  treatment at the Department of Ophthalmology,
  University of Leicester
- The Ulverscroft Vision Research Group,
  Institute of Child Health
- Twin operating theatres at the Western
  Ophthalmic Hospital, London
- The Chair of Ophthalmology at the Royal
  Australian College of Ophthalmologists

You can help further the work of the Foundation
by making a donation or leaving a legacy.
Every contribution is gratefully received. If you
would like to help support the Foundation or
require further information, please contact:

THE ULVERSCROFT FOUNDATION
The Green, Bradgate Road, Anstey
Leicester LE7 7FU, England
Tel: (0116) 236 4325

website: www.foundation.ulverscroft.com

THE PRICE OF FREEDOM

Liz Hargreaves has been a hostage for eight years when she is rescued by Spencer Ferguson, a newly appointed British consul. She is desperate to get home to her husband, David, and their daughters. But David had been told that Liz was dead, and started a relationship with Liz's best friend, Gillian, who is expecting David's baby. Gillian is as determined to hold on to David as Liz is to win him back, but there can only be one winner . . .

Books by Teresa Ashby
in the Linford Romance Library:

LOVE ON ICE
FOR THE CHILDREN'S SAKE
THE CALL OF HOME
A ONE-MAN WOMAN
FOOL'S PARADISE
CHERISH THE DREAM
WITHOUT A SHADOW OF DOUBT
TAKE A CHANCE ON ME
RUTH'S WAR
CORY'S GIRLS
SHACKLED TO THE PAST
THE GIRL FROM YESTERDAY
SEEK NEW HORIZONS
ANGEL'S TEARS
DOCTOR'S DECISION
ONE LAKELAND SUMMER

TERESA ASHBY

THE PRICE OF FREEDOM

Complete and Unabridged

LINFORD
Leicester

First published in Great Britain in 1994

First Linford Edition
published 2014

Copyright © 1994 by Teresa Ashby
All rights reserved

A catalogue record for this book is available
from the British Library.

ISBN 978–1–4448–2188–8

Published by
F. A. Thorpe (Publishing)
Anstey, Leicestershire

Set by Words & Graphics Ltd.
Anstey, Leicestershire
Printed and bound in Great Britain by
T. J. International Ltd., Padstow, Cornwall

This book is printed on acid-free paper

1

The woman stumbled as she emerged from her cell and fell to the floor, scrambling to her feet at once as one of the guards jabbed her between the shoulder blades with his gun. One thing she had learned was not to argue with a man who held a gun — and these men were obviously impatient to move her along.

She blinked in the half-light before she recognised the man standing in the shadows, waiting for her. He'd been to see her before and had promised to get her out, one way or another. He stepped forward when the guard jabbed her with his rifle again, but restrained himself from interfering. He didn't smile, but took her arm and supported her for the short walk to the outer door.

She stood for a moment, waiting, wondering; then the door clattered open and snagged on the rough, sandy earth outside. One of the guards kicked it, jarring it back on its rusted hinges. Fresh air gushed in, displacing the stale, stagnant atmosphere inside. He turned back and grunted at the woman to move.

Liz Hargreaves, given this chance of freedom, held back. She had thought, once the moment came — and she'd often prayed it would — that she'd be out of here like a shot, no turning back, just off and gone. But she stared at the rectangle of brilliant light ahead of her and hesitated, overcome by a nameless, faceless fear.

What if it were another of their cruel tricks? They hadn't played any of their games for some time, but perhaps her captors had become bored. Perhaps this man, who'd told her his name was Spencer Ferguson, wasn't really the British consul. Another thing she had learned was to trust no one. They hadn't carried out any of their mock executions for some time, but there had been such tension among the guards lately. She'd been handed from one set of captors to another over the years, and the latest ones didn't even seem to know why they were holding her. Perhaps they intended to march her out into the sunshine and be rid of her once and for all.

'Liz.' The man at her side stooped to speak to her. His voice was firm, confident, reassuring and, although the only word he spoke was her name, it gave her the push she needed to get her shaking legs moving again. She had to trust someone sometime, and now seemed as good a time as any.

Her long, straggly hair was tied back with a fraying piece of rag and her dark blue eyes looked huge in her wasted face. She felt frail and ragged, and was almost afraid to step into the light in case her body, unaccustomed to the rays of the sun, should turn to dust.

She was being irrational, foolish. She was a doctor; she knew better. But the fear was always there, and it wouldn't even begin to fade until she took those first faltering steps outside.

Limping, she took a couple of steps forward. Where a chain had dug into the flesh around her ankle, an infection had set in, making it painful to walk. She glanced to one side and saw another guard. They kept their faces hidden and all she ever saw of them was their eyes.

Now, the man who had told her his name was Spencer Ferguson, who had never hidden his face, who had given her his word that he would obtain her release, held tight to her hand. 'Are you all right?' he asked gently.

'Yes,' she whispered. She wanted to speak in a proper voice, but had been conditioned over the years only to speak when spoken to — and even then, only to whisper.

'Feeling a bit shaky?' He smiled and she clung to that smile. It was the first real smile she'd seen in so long . . . The only times her guards had ever shown their faces and smiled were . . . were too painful to remember. Smiles were to be feared; were often precursors to violence — and other terrors.

'You won't be needing those.' Spencer was speaking to the guards and Liz wanted to cry out, to warn him, that you don't tell these people what to do. He reached out, put his hand on the gun and calmly moved it aside. She cringed inside, waiting for the punishing blows, blinking, flinching, terrified — but nothing happened.

Spencer's hand tightened around hers and he spoke then to her captors in their own language. They replied in a barrage of words she only partially understood. They sounded angry. If things went wrong, they'd take it out on her, and she just wasn't sure she could take any more.

They were outside at last. Liz recoiled from the brightness. The sun was like thousands of sharp needles piercing her eyes. She put up her hand to shade them. How she'd longed to see the sun, and now she was almost cursing it. The light was really painful. It made her giddy and she stumbled.

Spencer's arm shot around her waist, immediately supporting her, keeping her upright, as they walked across the dusty ground towards his Land Rover. She looked up at the sky and the dizziness swam over her again. It looked so high, so far away, so blue that it terrified her. Everything was so huge out here. She felt small and insignificant and, despite her new freedom, it was as if the world were suddenly closing in all around her.

Spencer's driver was armed, Liz noticed. She shrank away from his gun, but Spencer's hold on her remained tight. 'Ahmed's a friend.' Then, to his driver, 'Let's get out of here before these people change their minds.'

'You're taking a stupid risk coming here,' Ahmed said, his voice tense as Spencer helped Liz into the rear seat. 'I thought you were never going to get out of that hell-hole. I told you . . . '

'Yes, yes, I know, Ahmed. Let's go, huh?'

Liz pressed herself into the corner of the back seat. She fought the urge to draw up her knees and hug them. *You don't have to be afraid any more,* a voice inside her head told her.

And then sweet reality began to sink in.

She was free. Turning, she looked out of the back of the car and saw the prison buildings fading into the distance. She was really free, and it had all happened so quickly. She'd never expected it to be like this. After years of captivity, she'd been so sure it would take months and months of negotiation to secure her release. And now it had really happened.

'What did he mean?' Liz whispered then.

'About what?'

'About the risk.'

'Ah.' Spencer smiled. 'The thing is, I'm still actually waiting for the official go-ahead to start negotiating for your release. But sometimes, time can be an enemy. I wanted to strike while the iron was hot, so,' he shrugged, 'I bent the rules a little.'

'Bent them,' Ahmed bellowed from the front of the car. 'You don't even know the rules. You should stick to building oil wells.'

'Ahmed and I go way back.' Spencer smiled again. 'We actually shared a flat for a while. Despite the way he carries on, we're good friends. I couldn't have asked anyone else to help me today.'

The car jogged and jolted over the bumpy surface. Liz clung to her seat. Her fingernails were broken, jagged and thinned by a combination of poor diet and lack of sunlight. Beside her, Spencer had been watching out of the back window, too, and now he turned to face the front, breathing a heavy sigh of relief.

'We're not being followed,' he said. 'So how does it feel to be free, Liz?'

'Free,' she whispered, still not able to believe she didn't have to whisper any more. 'Thank you . . . thank you for helping me. I — I just want to go home.' Her eyes filled with tears, stinging hot and cleansing. 'All I want is to go home and be with my family.'

* * *

'Gillian, will you please tell this girl that I'm not made of money?' David groaned in exasperation. 'It doesn't grow on trees, you know, love.'

Gillian sighed and picked up the cereal packet from the breakfast table. 'It is a good offer, David,' she said diplomatically. 'And if Emma wants to pay half . . . '

'Whose side are you on?' David laughed. 'You women, you're all the same, ganging up on a poor, defenceless male.'

'Dad, you didn't remind me about my maths revision last night,' Susie said. 'If I get rotten marks in my test, it'll be all your fault.'

'My fault?' David gasped. 'The girl doesn't do her homework and suddenly it's my fault.'

'It's OK, David, I went over it with her. She'll be fine. Mind the milk, Emma,' Gillian cried as the carton of milk toppled sideways. She grabbed it and righted it, but not in time to stop a stream running to the edge of the table and dripping onto the floor. 'Honestly. Why can't we be like those perfect families on the adverts?' Gillian muttered as she mopped up the milk. 'Look, there are cornflakes all over the place, and sugar, spilled tea . . . I think I'd rather serve breakfast to a bunch of chimps.'

'Do you girls want a lift to school?' David asked.

'All right, slave.' Susie grabbed her schoolbag. 'Get your car keys and let's go.'

'Got your lunches?' Gillian asked as they piled towards the door. She didn't know what it was about mornings, but there always seemed to be twice as many people in the house. Perhaps it was all the bags and paraphernalia they needed. Not that she'd change anything. She loved the hustle and bustle and the noise of a happy family.

'I'll be late tonight, Mum,' Susie said, kissing Gillian's cheek. 'Hockey practice. Joanne's mum will give me a lift home after.'

'Did you find your hockey socks?'

'In the airing cupboard,' Susie confirmed.

'Got your reading book, Em?'

'In my bag.'

Emma reached up to hug Gillian. 'Be good, darling,' Gillian said. 'Have a nice day.'

David watched, feeling a strange constriction around his heart. What would they do without Gillian? It didn't bear thinking about. 'Sorry about the mess,' David said, planting an affectionate kiss on top of Gillian's head. 'I'd stay and give you a hand, but . . . '

'Course you would.' She laughed and waited, waving on the doorstep, until David's car had turned the corner. Closing the door, she smiled to herself and looked at the phone. 'It's still too early,' she told herself firmly, then hurried back to the kitchen to tackle the clearing-up. The house always seemed so quiet and empty after they'd all gone. But, if all went well, she'd soon have more than enough to do, and the house certainly wouldn't be empty any more . . .

By nine o'clock, she couldn't wait a moment longer to call the doctor's surgery. Dr Steel was expecting her call. 'Gillian,' he said, 'I've just got in. Hold on for a moment.' She heard him rustling through some papers on his desk and was aware she was holding her breath. Her fingers were tightly crossed and she was counting slowly to ten. She could hardly bear the suspense. She'd waited so long for this, hoping and praying, and now . . .

The telephone crackled as the doctor picked it up again at the other end. 'Gillian, you still there, m'dear?'

'Yes.'

'It's good news. I've got your test result right here and, yes, you're definitely pregnant.'

'Oh.' Gillian sank into the chair beside the phone. 'Oh, Doctor, thank you, thank you.'

'Nothing to do with me, m'dear.' He chuckled mischievously. 'I just deliver the good news. Congratulations anyway. I told you those home tests are never wrong!'

But she hadn't dared believe the tests she'd done at home, certain that there had been a mistake. Dr Steel, knowing how much she longed for a child, had indulged her.

'Thank you,' she said again. Tears welled up in her eyes and fell like rain onto her cheeks; tears of pure happiness.

'Now, then, I'll put you through to reception and you can make an appointment to attend the antenatal clinic. I'll also see if I can get you in for a scan as quickly as possible, just to give you more accurate dates and to reassure you that everything will be fine.'

Bless the man. He knew how worried she was.

'Gillian . . . ? Are you there, dear?'

'I'm still here, Doctor,' she said softly.

'You are all right, aren't you?'

'Oh, yes, but — but I'm just so happy,' she said, and burst into tears all over again. 'I'm over the moon.' Although she loved Susie and Emma as if they were her own flesh and blood, Gillian had longed to have a child with David, a child of their own — and soon, before time ran out.

Now, it seemed, her dream was to come true.

* * *

They'd left the parched, arid, dusty land behind and were now entering a more fertile area. Liz looked out of the window wonderingly at the trees and the birds. Their colours were all so bright, so vibrant, that even looking at the grass made her eyes sting. Was this how it felt to have been blind and to see once more?

14

'We're some way across the border now, Liz,' Spencer said. 'But we've still a long way to go, a lot of miles to cover. Would you like to stop somewhere for a drink?'

A drink. Something as simple as a drink and she had a choice? She could say yes or no and, if she said yes, then she could choose what to have.

'We'll stop,' Spencer said, understanding her bewilderment. 'Whenever you like, Liz. I'll call the embassy as well, and let them know what's happening.'

★   ★   ★

The small hotel was friendly and cool inside. Huge ceiling fans spun overhead. Best of all, it was virtually empty.

Liz sank gratefully into a chair. She'd deliberately chosen a place well away from the window where she could sit in a corner with her back pressed against the wall. Ahmed had gone off to deal with some business of his own. 'How long has he worked for you?' Liz asked.

'He doesn't work for me,' Spencer laughed. 'He's a physicist, actually — and quite brilliant.' Spencer looked round for a phone and saw one in the lobby beside the lounge. 'I'll be just over there,' he told Liz, pointing to the telephone. 'I won't be out of sight for a second. You'll be all right?'

'Yes,' she said in a normal voice, and flinched. It sounded so loud inside her own head that she wondered if she'd shouted. 'I'll order coffee. Is coffee all right? Or could I have tea?'

'You can have whatever you like.' He grinned. 'Relax, Liz. You're safe now. We're over the border. No one can touch you now.'

She watched him all the time he was on the phone. A lot of the time he seemed to be listening. Occasionally, he'd throw up his hand and raise his voice a little and once, just once, she saw him hunch his shoulders and kick at the carpet, like a small child getting a telling-off. It made her smile, and smiling felt so strange. Her face didn't seem to want to smile, as if all the muscles had wasted through lack of use.

When Spencer returned, he was grinning. 'Right, we're all set,' he said. 'The Foreign Office is delighted with your release and a pot of tea is on the way.'

'But?' She smiled.

He laughed. 'You smiled. Well done, Liz. It suits you. Anyway, more importantly, I've just set the wheels in motion for your return home. Basically, you'll be flown to a British air base for debriefing. I've asked them to keep it pretty low profile. In the past, hostages came home to huge press coverage, but, well, to be frank . . . '

'No one back home even remembers Dr Liz Hargreaves,' she said. 'I gathered as much. At first, there were one or two visits from officials who said they were doing all they could.' Her voice cracked a little, but she went on. 'They obviously felt it would be better to keep quiet about me. I wasn't important or well known. Perhaps the Foreign Office thought that, by playing it down, I'd be released all the quicker. Then they moved me, handed me over to another group, and I never saw or spoke to anyone . . . '

'You weren't forgotten, Liz,' he said vehemently. 'When I first took up my post out here, I found out about you and, well, I made it my business to look into your disappearance and try to find out what had happened to you. I had a feeling you were still alive, despite the reports of your death.'

She smiled. 'I'm very glad you did.'

'We're going to make it up to you now. As I speak, they're booking you into a five-star hotel just until all the arrangements for your return home are completed. You'll have a suite of rooms, a bath . . . '

'A bath?' she echoed.

'Every comfort possible. Liz. No expense spared.'

She shook her head. 'No, I'm sorry. No. I can't.'

'Can't? What do you mean, Liz? We're talking the very best hotels here.

It'll be like heaven after what you've been used to.'

She shivered, wrapped her arms around herself and stared at the teapot. 'Don't get me wrong,' she said. 'I don't mean to sound ungrateful, but . . . all those people. I couldn't, Spencer. I'd be terrified. So many strangers.' Suddenly, her hand shot out and she gripped his arm fearfully with bony white fingers, her huge eyes now staring at him, her former shaky composure all but gone. 'Please, don't make me stay in a hotel. You're the first British person I've spoken to in years and years. I wouldn't know how to cope. Isn't there somewhere else I could stay? What about your place? Couldn't I stay there? With you.'

'There's not a lot of room,' he said evasively. 'It's just a small place really. I do have a spare room, but . . . '

'Please, Spencer,' she pleaded.

★ ★ ★

The apartment was really quite large, but Spencer still felt uneasy about having Liz to stay with him. Part of him believed he should be firm, follow the official line, book her into the hotel and leave her to the small army of waiting doctors. But another part saw her for what she was: a frightened, vulnerable woman, just about ready to fall apart. And he couldn't deny her the right to feel safe, not after all she'd been through. As he was in enough trouble already for going ahead and fetching her, he couldn't see that having her to stay in his apartment would make things much worse.

It didn't make the slightest difference, of course, that he'd been successful. The F.O. would still bombard him with what-ifs and come down on him with a multitude of international rights and wrongs.

He watched her now as she moved about the living-room, looking at things, touching things. She even let the curtains slide through her fingers.

Sensing him watching, she turned to face him. 'I'm sorry. It's like I'm seeing it all for the first time. I've felt nothing but concrete floors and rough, stinking mattresses for so long. It's wonderful to feel something soft and clean again.'

'How about that bath then?' He grinned. 'There's plenty of hot water.'

'Hot water,' she breathed incredulously. 'Oh, Spencer, you don't know how I've longed for a bath to wash all this dirt and grime away.'

'And while you're soaking in the tub, I'll get us something to eat.'

'Nothing too rich,' she said, the nutritionist in her automatically coming to the fore, even after all these years. She'd like nothing better than to tuck into a huge meal, but she knew that if she did, she'd probably end up making herself ill.

'I understand,' he said. 'Right, the bathroom's through there. There are clean towels in the cupboard and my robe's hanging on the door. Feel free to use whatever you like.'

She looked at her reflection in the bathroom mirror for a long, long time. It was like looking at the face of a complete stranger. Her hair, once a warm, soft brown, was now streaked with grey; her skin was an unhealthy colour, and there were lines of strain and anxiety etched around her eyes. Tentatively, she reached up to touch her face with shaking fingers. She looked so different, but she felt the same. Deep down inside, she was still Liz Hargreaves. No matter what else they'd done to her, they could never strip her of her identity.

Unable to face herself a moment longer, she turned from the mirror and stood beside the bath, A tear slid down her cheek and dripped into the water. After all these years, the longing to be with her loved ones had never been as strong as it was at this moment. Now that she could let herself believe she really would see them again, the longing became an ache, a burning pain deep inside.

She was on her way home.

★ ★ ★

Liz sat down at the table, her damp hair curling as it dried, her thin, frail body swamped by Spencer's bathrobe. Minus the grime, she looked delicate and he found it hard to imagine that this woman had been through so much and survived.

'It's just rice and chicken,' he said apologetically. 'Very plain and simple.'

'After the mush I've eaten, it looks delicious.' She ate slowly, savouring every mouthful, fighting back the urge to bolt the food. It helped having Spencer there to talk to.

'The information I have on you is very sketchy,' he said. 'What were you doing out here? How did you manage to get yourself kidnapped?'

'I came out just for a month,' she said softly. 'I saw a report on the news about the plight of some of the children here and I knew I could help them. I looked at my kids . . . I looked at them and I thought, every child should be warm and secure and properly fed. As a paediatrician and nutritionist, I wanted to use my skills to help people. I didn't want to commit myself for longer than a month, though.' She laughed ironically. 'I thought a month was more than enough time to be parted from my family. Actually, my husband wasn't keen on my coming out here at all, but it was something I simply had to do.' Her eyes closed and creased with pain at the memory. 'I was two days away from coming home when I was invited to speak at a small medical conference. I guess the car sent to pick me up looked pretty important. I can't think why else it was run off the road. I'd grown pretty used to seeing guns out here, but I'd never had one pushed into my face before. If I'd known what lay ahead, Spencer, I'd have risked death to get away from them.'

She fell silent and put her fork down on her plate. A clock ticked loudly somewhere in the apartment and Spencer felt compelled to say something to break the silence, but he didn't know what. Knowing the right things to say was for the experts and he was just an ordinary man, sitting at his table with a very extraordinary woman. Finally, he asked, 'Was it really awful?' A stupid question, he knew, but it was all he could think to say in the deepening silence.

'At times it was pure hell,' she said, looking at him with all the raw hurt and pain and sheer agony of years evident in her eyes. 'I was kept with other women now and again, but they didn't speak English . . . ' She broke off. 'I'm sorry.' She shook her head. 'I can't.'

'Of course not,' he said, his voice thick. It was the invisible scars that would never heal, and they were also the most painful.

'I can't eat any more,' she said, pushing her plate away, feeling nauseous and full.

'Would you like anything else? Some fruit, perhaps?'

She shook her head. 'Not at the moment.'

'Liz . . . '

'I'm all right, Spencer. It's just, talking about it for the first time, you know. I keep thinking someone's going to kick me and wake me up. I've dreamed so many times of being free, of being back with my family again. It's all I've lived for these past years. I must have come close to death several times, but I fought back, not because I'm strong or anything like that, but because I wanted to see my family again. Death would have been an escape, a way out, and sometimes I longed for it. But then I'd have a vision of my family and I'd want, more than anything else, to live. I was damned if I was going to die in some foreign country and lose them for ever.'

She took a deep breath and went on. 'All I want is to go home now and be with them. My elder daughter was four when I left; the little one was just two. They thought it was a great adventure, you know — Mummy going off to a foreign country and my friend moving in to look after them for a whole month. It must have seemed like a lifetime, though, to them. Little did we all know . . . It really seems like a lifetime . . . '

'They don't even know that you're free yet,' he said. 'They've that joy to come. If I'd gone through the proper channels, they'd have been waiting at home for news, possibly even been flown out to meet you somewhere along the way. But I couldn't wait for officialdom to get its act together. There was a possibility that you were going to be passed to yet another group, and then I could have lost you. That's why I had to act quickly.'

'Thank God you did,' she said sincerely, softly, knowing she owed everything to him.'

* * *

The rocket, when it came, wasn't as bad as Spencer had been expecting.

'But don't ever think of trying to pull a stunt like that again, Ferguson. Next time it could go wrong and you could end up as a hostage yourself — or worse. You can't take risks out here. The situation is too volatile. And it wasn't even in this country. I mean, how on earth did you get her across the border? No . . . no, don't tell me. I don't think I want to know. Others will, though. I'm sure it was illegal. Anyway, what made you think you could go swanning off, ignoring borders, trampling diplomatic procedure underfoot? That's what rules are for — to protect ourselves. You're new to consulship. Let me remind you that your duties are to take care of the commercial interests of our citizens, not to dash around all over the place like some maverick righting wrongs. You really must stick to the rules.'

Spencer looked across the desk to where three senior embassy staff sat, like a row of judiciary in solemn judgement, contemplating him with stern faces.

'Oh dear. Stole someone's thunder, did I?'

The remark was ignored. 'Has Doctor Hargreaves seen a medical officer yet?'

'Yes, first thing this morning. She's being treated for an infection in her foot, that's all. But I think she'll probably need some therapy, too. So what's the form? What happens now?' he asked.

'Doctor Hargreaves will be taken for debriefing and she'll need a thorough medical examination.'

'I think,' Spencer interrupted, 'that any medicals should be carried out by women, as far as possible. She let a male doctor examine her foot this morning, but it was obvious she was far from happy about it.'

'What do you take us for? We're not fools. We know what happens to women in these jails.'

'What about her family? I gather

there's only her husband and kids,' Spencer said. 'Any news about them?'

'I'm afraid that we've had some difficulty in locating her family. They've moved on from the last known address. But we've got people working on it. It's only a matter of time.'

'Moved on?' Spencer said in disbelief. 'What do you mean, moved on? How could they move and not let anyone know?'

'Remember, for years, nothing was heard of Elizabeth Hargreaves. She might have been dead for all we knew. Her husband started a campaign for her release, but we persuaded him that it might not be in her best interests to continue. A media campaign may well have had the opposite effect, giving the hostage undue importance, making them even more determined to hang on to her.'

'Didn't work, though, did it?' Spencer remarked drily.

'We hadn't heard of her for more than four years, Ferguson. We don't have the facilities or the manpower to carry out lengthy investigations. We'd even been told that she was dead. But since there was nothing to substantiate it, we had to ignore that information — wisely, as it happens.'

Spencer was about to make a cutting remark, but held back. He wasn't going to do himself or Liz Hargreaves any good at all by losing his cool. If there was one thing he hated, it was red tape, especially when lives were at stake.

'If that's all, gentlemen,' he said, 'I'll get back to my office.' He had another long drive ahead of him from the embassy to his small office in a port several miles away. Normally, he dealt with the problems of British nationals who had been robbed, or had lost their money and passports, or he sorted out problems for British citizens working in the area. It was a part-time position, fitted in around his real business as the head of an engineering outfit. He rarely had much to do with the embassy itself. He'd been quite pleased at first to be appointed as British consul, but it wasn't half as exciting as it sounded.

At least, it hadn't been until that moment he'd keyed into the database and seen Liz Hargreaves's name. That, for him, was when the job had really started.

*   *   *

Before going back to work, Spencer checked his apartment and found Liz still sleeping. She was exhausted and had got up long enough to eat a light breakfast and see the doctor before going back to bed. He watched her for a moment. Even in sleep, she looked troubled. He thought of a photograph taken of her before her captivity. Something about that picture had captivated him, firing his imagination. She'd looked so vibrant, so alive and so young . . .

It was going to take a long time for her to get over this, if she ever did.

Locking the apartment behind him, he went down to his office. Getting straight down to work, he keyed in to his computer. Spencer always preferred the direct approach and it didn't take him long to find what he was looking for.

The previous consul had kept a file on Liz Hargreaves and had updated it quite recently. Liz really hadn't been forgotten and Spencer's predecessor had tried all he could to find her without success.

'Ah,' he said, as the information he required appeared in the database, 'here we are.' It was exactly what he was looking for. Liz Hargreaves's husband had moved to a completely new area. Formerly a science teacher at a large state school, he now owned and ran his own business, The Old Barn Workshop. It couldn't have been easy setting up a new business in the depths of a recession, Spencer thought. Then he read on, his frown deepening until it turned into an expression of anger as the full story unfolded before his eyes.

He swore and thumped his desk in frustration. This was the last thing he expected to find.

It was quiet and cool in the workshop. David sat in the office, tapping a pad of paper with a pencil. He was meant to be phoning an order through, but he had so much on his mind, he was finding it difficult to concentrate.

He'd had such dreams, such hopes, but they seemed to be turning to dust before his eyes.

Sometimes, he thought he must have been crazy to give up a steady job, especially to run a business like this. In a recession, any business was bound to do badly; but if people had antiques requiring restoration, that would be low on their list of priorities when it came to spending money.

And yesterday, he'd had the news that he was to be a father again. A new baby would be wonderful, welcomed and loved, but it would also be a financial burden. The thought made him feel guilty. Gillian wanted to have a child while she still could and he had no right to deny her that joy. He was happy about it too, but life had taught him that nothing is ever easy.

'Don't look so glum, David,' Roy, the lad he'd taken on as a school-leaver, said. 'We're breaking even.'

'You're right.' David smiled. 'Making a fortune will come later, eh?'

'You're not telling me that you're doing this to make a fortune.' Roy laughed. 'I don't believe that for a minute. I've watched you work. You love what you do.'

'Right again.' David's smile widened. 'I should count my blessings really. This beats standing up in front of a bunch of stroppy teenagers any day. I've never yet had a Windsor chair give me any lip.'

'Hey,' Roy said, 'I'm a teenager, but I'm not stroppy.'

'Present company excepted,' David said, turning to the window. A large black car had drawn up outside and David leaned forward to get a better look. He whistled softly.

'What is it?' Roy joined him. 'Customers, do you think?'

David shrugged as two men got out of the car. 'They don't look like customers,' he said.

'No, they look like policemen,' Roy muttered. 'You haven't been fiddling your tax returns, have you?'

David grimaced. 'Well, whoever they are, they're coming in here. Call that order through for me, would you, Roy? I think I'd better deal with them.'

'Aye, aye, boss,' Roy said, clipping his heels together and saluting.

David left his assistant in the small office and went to the front of the workshop, an odd tightness in his stomach. He was sure they weren't customers. They looked far too official. Surely Roy wasn't right that he'd fallen foul of the Revenue? He'd always been very careful to do things properly.

'Good morning, gentlemen,' he said as they entered the workshop. His cheerfulness was forced and he hoped it didn't show. 'What can I do for you?'

'We're looking for Mr David Hargreaves.'

'That's my name above the door,' he said lightly, but the men were very serious and he added, 'I'm David Hargreaves. What's wrong?'

'It's about your wife, Mr Hargreaves.'

'My wife?' His mouth went dry. As far as he knew, his wife, his common-law wife, was at home. He was suddenly gripped by a terrible fear. If anything had happened to Gillian, he didn't know how he'd cope. A hundred things flashed through his mind. What if she'd lost the baby . . . or had an accident? If she lost the baby, it would destroy her. She — they — wanted it so much.

'What's happened? Is Gillian all right?'

'Gillian? You are David Hargreaves?'

'Yes, yes,' David said impatiently. Surely to God tragedy wasn't about to strike him again? Hadn't he and the girls had enough? He was aware of his heart thundering and found it hard to breathe.

'You are married to Doctor Elizabeth Hargreaves?'

'Liz? You mean there's news — after all this time?'

'Yes, Mr Hargreaves, there is news. That's why we're here.'

2

David Hargreaves paced from one side of the small room to the other, aware that Spencer Ferguson, sitting on the edge of a small table, was watching his every move.

'Why don't you sit down, David?' Spencer suggested. 'It won't be long now.'

David stopped and rubbed his eyes. They felt sore and gritty from lack of sleep. The past week had seen his mood rocketing between elation and depression and, right now, he felt wedged somewhere between the two. He'd hoped to get things straight in his mind on the flight over, but he was still as confused as ever.

Liz was alive. Yet, he still couldn't believe it — wouldn't believe it — until he saw her with his own eyes.

He'd wanted to fly out to meet her

straight away, but had been advised to wait until Liz had been thoroughly debriefed, and then it had all been a rush. For the past week, a team of R.A.F. doctors and psychiatrists had been taking care of her.

'What sort of shape is she in — mentally, I mean?' he asked.

'She's in surprisingly good shape,' Spencer told him. 'Considering . . . '

'Why didn't they let her go in the first place?' David groaned. 'All those years ago when they first discovered she wasn't anyone important?'

Spencer shrugged. 'I doubt if we'll ever know,' he said. 'For the most part, she was held by minor, often unknown factions. Basically, her captors were little more than a succession of political extremists. Sometimes, the groups themselves don't even seem to know what they're about.'

'God,' David whispered, pressing his fingers hard into his forehead. 'Poor Liz.'

'The medics have treated her for a

few physical ailments,' Spencer went on coolly. 'And she's responding well. She's a very remarkable woman; I've never met anyone with such determination.'

David smiled. He felt proud of Liz. If anyone could come through all this, she could. But his smile was quick to fade. 'Mr Ferguson . . . Spencer . . . I — does Liz know that I have a new home and . . . and a new woman in my life?'

Spencer stiffened. He'd been very friendly, helping David through the red tape, talking to him, making him feel at ease, preparing him for this critical meeting with his wife, but now he looked distinctly uneasy. 'No, she doesn't,' he said at last. 'On top of . . . No, all things considered, the team felt it would be best coming from you.' He looked away as if he couldn't bear to meet David's eyes.

David felt uncomfortable. Spencer didn't have to voice his disapproval and distaste. It was all there, written on his face. In an effort to stop his hands shaking, David clasped them together. 'Spencer, I . . . '

But before he could continue, the outer door opened and Liz walked into the room. Spencer slipped out, unnoticed, by the same door.

David hadn't seen Liz for nearly eight years. At times he'd forgotten what she looked like, but here she was at last, standing before him. She looked smaller than he remembered somehow, vulnerable, and he longed to reach out and hold her. She'd walked into the room confidently enough, but now she seemed frightened, shy almost, and her hands were shaking. Her hair was longer, he noticed, and shot with grey, and her face was more sculptured. But, underneath all that, she hadn't really changed. She was still the woman he'd fallen in love with, and seeing her like this had brought it all rushing back. She'd been through hell, but she was still beautiful. As he looked into her eyes, he was aware instantly of that indefinable something he'd never found in any other woman.

There was so much he wanted to say, so many things he had to tell her; but now the moment had come, he was struck dumb.

Liz, too, felt so confused and uncertain. For almost eight years, this was what had kept her determined to stay alive — this moment, seeing David again. In all that time, there had been only him and the girls to fill her thoughts. She'd imagined this moment a million times and had always known exactly what she'd say and do. But now the time was here, she was rooted to the spot, too scared to move in case she should stumble and fall over. She'd imagined herself running into his arms and him holding her, then going home and everything being all right.

But now she wasn't sure what to do. Their relationship had always been strongly spiritual as well as physical so that, often, they had no need for words. But eight years was a long time . . .

She could feel her heart banging,

hear her pulse thundering in her ears. She felt hot and cold all at once and experienced a rush of sudden, unexpected fear, like a young girl on a first big date.

I love you. Your love kept me alive all this time. The words echoed inside her head, but wouldn't come out.

She met his eyes slowly and saw the old love still there. Words filled her mind, but she couldn't speak.

Thanks for waiting for me, David . . . I love you, I love you . . .

'David,' she whispered at last. 'This is so silly, isn't it?'

They took a tentative step towards each other and hugged awkwardly. David kissed her, then he laughed nervously and held her at arm's length, looking at her all over again. The first feelings of awkwardness had been overcome, but they both still felt strange.

'I can't get over how great you look, Liz,' he said at last. 'I thought you'd have changed beyond recognition after all this time.'

'You look pretty good yourself,' she choked. 'You've got your hair shorter now. It suits you, and . . . and you've put on a little weight, but you're still you, David.'

He was still holding her hands, and in a reactive gesture he lifted one to his lips and kissed it, watching her all the time.

She closed her eyes as his lips softly brushed the back of her hand. She had feared she'd recoil from his touch — from any touch — but she didn't. She welcomed physical contact that brought only love and warmth, not terror and pain. 'I've missed you so much David,' she whispered. 'And Susie . . . and Emma . . . Did they come with you?'

'No.' He avoided her gaze for the first time since they'd met. He couldn't bear to see the hope in her eyes. 'We thought it might be a bit traumatic for them.'

We?

'How are they? Tell me all about them, David. How tall is Emma? Did

45

she shoot up like we thought she would? Does Susie still ride? Oh, David, there's so much I want to know. What do they look like now? They'll have changed so much. Emma was just a toddler last time I saw her.'

David delved into the inside pocket of his jacket. 'I brought some photos.'

She snatched them eagerly as he passed them to her, but her grip failed and they fluttered to the floor. 'I'm so clumsy,' she cried, putting up her hands. 'I'm sorry, David. I will get better — I will. I won't always be like this.'

She spoke with such fierce determination, it hurt to hear her. He picked up the photographs. 'Sit down, love,' he said gently. 'I'll pass them to you one at a time.'

Meekly, she allowed him to lead her to a chair. He'd never seen this side of her before. Never known her to do anything she was told. He'd seen so many different people over the past few days, and one of them had said he'd find she'd had the stuffing knocked out of her. At first glance, he'd thought they were wrong; but as he looked at her sitting on the chair, small and vulnerable, he now knew the truth of those words.

He watched as Liz looked through the pictures, studying each one intently, trying to take in every detail. She blinked back tears and he knew then that she really was stronger than anyone had ever given her credit for. She was holding herself together, no matter how much effort it took.

'Do they like school?'

'Love it.'

'Have they lots of friends?'

'Dozens. The house is always full of kids.'

'They're so beautiful . . . I never dreamed my girls would grow up to be so beautiful. Well, yes, I did, but . . . It feels so strange to be seeing them so grown up.'

He perched on the table, watching her as she went through the photographs again and again. At last, with obvious reluctance, she handed them back. 'Keep them,' he said, and her eyes lit up like a small child's as she clutched them against her chest.

'Oh, thanks, David, thanks a lot. I could look at them all day,' she said with a nervous smile. 'So, tell me all about yourself. Eight years is a long time. Are you still teaching?'

'No.' He looked away again, ashamed not to be able to meet her eyes as directly as she met his. 'I've got my own business now, The Old Barn Workshop, it's called. I restore antiques.'

'Is it doing well?'

'I'm holding up. You can't ask for more than that these days, Liz. There's a recession on. You won't know anything about that.' He reached out and took both her hands in his, cupping them inside. 'I never forgot you, you have to know that. At first, we campaigned non-stop for your release. We pestered the press, but it was rumoured that you'd been arrested and charged — something to do with illegal drugs.'

She gasped.

'No, no,' he said quickly. 'We knew that wasn't true. The embassy heard you were still alive . . . then you disappeared, vanished without a trace. We were advised — or maybe instructed would be the right word — to drop the campaign. Unofficial sources later confirmed that you were dead. God, we were even shown grainy photographs of a body and told it was you.' His voice cracked. 'We didn't give up, though, not even then. But the years passed and we heard nothing. Other hostages came back and none had ever heard of you. We were convinced you were dead, Liz. We even held a memorial service in St Luke's.'

'Oh, David, how awful for you,' Liz said, taking on the role of comforter now, as tears slid unchecked down her husband's cheeks. 'Poor darling. I'm so sorry for putting you through all that.' She gently wiped away his tears with her fingers. 'I know you did all you could,' she said firmly. 'I don't blame you for giving up. In a way, it must have been worse for you than it was for me. You and the kids. But it was you that got me through it, David. Whether you realised it or not, it was only the thought that one day I'd be back with you all again that kept me going.'

David moved away from the table, away from Liz. He felt devastated knowing what he had to do.

'But they say you've moved house now,' she went on, trying to lighten the atmosphere. 'Was that for your business? Or . . . what?'

David opened his mouth to explain. He'd wondered how he was ever going to get round to telling Liz that he had set up home with someone else, that Gillian was expecting his child, but she was handing him the opportunity on a plate.

'Liz, I . . . '

'You must have had a lot of help from our friends,' she said suddenly. 'I often thought about how you'd cope, but I knew they'd rally round, especially Gillian. She was always great in a crisis.

If I ever started to really worry about how you were all coping, I'd think of Gill.'

David felt physically sick. He'd never quite felt this way before but, right now, he didn't like himself very much. Liz had been through hell and now he was going to put her through it again — a very different sort of hell. Just when she should have been recovering, he was going to have to knock her back. Yet it had to be done, and he was the only one to do it.

'Liz,' he said, his voice hoarse, 'listen, love. There's something you have to know . . . It's about Gillian . . . and me.'

* * *

David rushed from the room, leaving the door to swing shut behind him. Spencer jumped to his feet, ready to speak, but David pushed past, obviously very upset. 'She knows,' he grated. 'All of it. Everything.'

Spencer looked at the door, then at David's retreating back and, with his usual impulsiveness, rushed into the room. The doctors would probably have advised him to leave Liz alone for a while, to come to terms with the news, but he couldn't bear to think of her coping alone. He stormed in and she looked up.

'You knew about this, Spencer?' she asked softly.

He nodded. He'd expected to find her in floods of tears, in pieces. This was worse. If only she would cry.

'I just don't know what to think,' she said. 'I feel . . . I feel numb at the moment. Gillian and I, we'd been friends for years. I can't believe that she and David . . . '

He moved closer and took her hand. He'd done a lot of that over the past week and she seemed to draw a lot of comfort from that one small physical contact. 'It'll take a while to sink in,' he said softly. 'But, if it's any help, it's not as if they deliberately set out to hurt you. Remember, they'd been told that you were dead.'

'I know,' she said.

'I have something else to tell you that may help a little,' Spencer said. 'It was confirmed this morning that I'm flying back home with you. I'll be there to help you with some of the pressures you'll be facing. We've kept this as low-key as possible, but it's inevitable that the press will find out — and natural, I suppose, that they'll want to know what's happened.'

'The press?' She seemed to shrink and he tightened his hold on her hand.

'Don't worry,' he said firmly. 'I'll be there if the media guys are a problem. We'll simply move you to a safe house for a while until the fuss dies down. I think press attention is going to be the least of your worries, though,' Spencer said forthrightly. 'I've already seen how strong you are. But Liz, how will you handle this situation? Your husband and your best friend, I mean?'

She considered for a long while

before speaking. When she did reply, Spencer saw that spark he'd often seen in her eyes in the short time he'd known her. She had to be something special to have come through the past eight years.

'I don't know for sure,' she said. 'I feel as if I've gone straight from one nightmare into another. But . . . ' She paused for a moment, looked directly at Spencer and went on. 'I'll cope. Somehow, I'll cope.'

* * *

'Here we are,' David said unnecessarily as the plane touched down. They were at an R.A.F. airbase in Wiltshire but, as far as Liz was concerned, they might have been anywhere on the planet. She sat for a moment, staring into space. Only yesterday, David had broken the news about his relationship with Gillian. But Liz had thought about it so much, she felt as if she had known forever.

'Look, Liz.' Spencer leaned across and pointed out of the window.

Slowly, she turned her head and saw the small crowd waiting. 'Susie . . . Emma . . . ?' She brightened visibly.

Spencer shook his head and looked at David. 'You'll see the girls at home,' he said. 'Right, do you feel ready to face the journalists? Or shall I try to get rid of them?'

'Oh, I may as well face them.' She smiled. 'Get it over and done with once and for all.' She stood up, staggering slightly. 'Sorry,' she apologised. 'I'm still a bit unsteady on my feet.'

The door was opened and, holding tightly to Spencer's arm, Liz drew in her breath sharply.

That smell. Home. The night sky was laced with mist, the air damp and slightly musty, but it was home. After the arid daytime heat she'd been used to and the bitterly cold nights, this was like heaven.

She stopped for a moment at the top of the steps and waved. Why were all these people here? she wondered. She wasn't anyone important, just a hard-working doctor who'd happened to be in the wrong place at the wrong time.

David held back, letting Liz and Spencer go down the steps ahead to meet the barrage of flashing lights and shouted questions. An official from the Foreign Office stepped forward and made a small speech. Liz didn't hear a word, but nodded numbly. She didn't like the flashing lights and flinched away from them. Spencer, feeling her discomfort, put his arm protectively about her shoulders.

She couldn't take any of it in. All she could think about was Gillian at home with her children, sleeping with her husband, expecting his baby.

'Are you glad to be home, Dr Hargreaves?'

'What did you miss most of all?'

'What were your first words to your husband?'

'What were the conditions like?'

Her head spun and she allowed

Spencer to hustle her forward and away from the shouting journalists. David hung back, answering questions, giving Spencer a chance to get Liz away and safely inside the building.

'What happens now?' Liz asked.

'You'll stay here tonight and there'll be another medical assessment tomorrow morning. After that, if the doctors give you the go-ahead, you can go home. The story we'll be giving to the press is that you and David are going to a safe house in Cornwall.'

'And that's it?'

'Far from it,' he said. 'You're a doctor, Liz. You know the score. You'll need further treatment and assessments, and possibly protection for some time from that pack of hounds out there.'

Later, as Liz sat on the edge of her bed in the basic R.A.F. quarters, she stared again at the photographs David had given her. She'd been there with her daughters every step of the way, but only in her mind. She'd imagined

Emma's first day at school, seeing David walking her in through the school gate.

Now, whenever she thought about it, Gillian was the one she saw holding Emma's hand.

Birthdays, Christmases — she'd been with them every time in spirit even though she had no idea of the date, but had they thought of her at all? Or had Gillian been so good at playing surrogate mother that they hadn't even missed her? And there were the times she knew nothing about: the childhood illnesses when only a hug from Mum would do the trick — and she hadn't been there to give it.

If it had been anyone else but Gillian . . . but somehow the fact that her own best friend had stepped so neatly into her shoes was the most painful of all to bear.

She stood up. 'They're my kids,' she said aloud. 'My kids and my husband. I'm not giving them up. Not for anyone.'

To do so would make a mockery of

all she'd endured. David used to say she was like a tigress when it came to her children. She'd die for them. David, too. She remembered how he'd looked at her when they'd met the day before. The expression on his face had spoken volumes. He obviously hadn't forgotten how good they'd been together.

A small smile crossed her face. They'd had some terrible rows, it was true, but making up afterwards had always been fun. There had never been any shortage of love or passion in their stormy relationship. She could win him back, she was sure . . .

Her shoulders slumped and she sank back down onto the bed. But how could she when she wasn't the same person? The things that had happened to her had changed her. But David was still the same; he had to be.

'When will I really be free?' she whispered.

She'd thought she'd feel free when she was released, when Spencer helped her take her first faltering steps into the outside world. But it hadn't happened then, and she waited for it still with a kind of childish expectation, a sudden sense of freedom that never came.

Ironically, she now felt more trapped than ever before, and more helpless.

Before, she'd been fighting to survive, taking one day at a time with one goal in mind. Now, the enemy was very different. But she was no less determined to put up the fight of her life — for the survival of her family.

*　*　*

Gillian and the girls watched the news in silence. There was a very brief item about the arrival home of a hostage few people had ever heard of and a small snatch of film.

David appeared briefly, looking tired and careworn, long enough to say, 'Yes, of course I'm glad to have Liz home. It's been a long time. We just want to be left in peace with our children to pick up the pieces of our lives.'

Gillian, Susie and Emma stared at the TV screen as the newsreader went on to talk about the day's fog and the spate of accidents it had caused across the country.

'Well.' Gillian got to her feet and switched off the set. 'At least we know they're back safely.' She'd caught only a glimpse of Liz being helped off the plane. She couldn't help wondering how David had felt when he'd seen Liz again.

Liz had always been so dynamic, so right for him. As a couple, Gillian had always felt that the chemistry between them was something almost tangible. Liz was vital and alive and had an extra little something that made her extremely attractive. What some would call sex appeal. Certainly, when David and Liz had been together, they were always touching. It was as if David couldn't keep his hands off her. And his eyes would follow her everywhere she went, as if he couldn't bear to let her out of his sight, even for a moment.

Memories like this had been haunting her all week. But now that Liz was back, definitely back, these thoughts rose up like a giant beast to confront her and remind her of her own lack of confidence.

David had spoken of bringing her home and picking up the pieces. What did that mean, exactly? She'd asked him on the phone where Liz would go and he'd replied, 'Well, home with us of course. Where else is there?'

'I think you should go to bed now,' she said, realising that the girls had been watching her very closely. 'You've had a busy day. You must be tired out.'

She'd taken them riding, as much to occupy her own thoughts as the girls'. They'd had a lovely day, but Gillian's thoughts had never been far from Liz and David. The girls were looking at her and she suddenly felt very frightened. She'd been a mother to them for years now and she'd cherished every minute of it. How ironic that, when she and David were going to have a child of their own, Liz should come back.

She reached out and hugged them both, knowing she couldn't bear to lose either of them. 'Goodnight,' she said, kissing them in turn. 'Try to get some sleep. I know it's difficult, but I really want you to be rested for tomorrow.'

'Will Dad bring Mum home, do you think?' Susie asked. 'They said on the news that she'd be taken to a safe house.'

Gillian nodded. She couldn't trust herself to speak. It seemed so odd to hear Susie refer to someone else as Mum. Gillian would never have let the girls call her Mum unless she'd been one hundred per cent sure that Liz was dead. It had been a dreadful step to take, finally accepting that Liz wouldn't be coming back, but it had changed everything.

Emma's mouth set in a grim line. 'You're our mum — not her.'

Gillian hugged them again. She could see from Susie's face that she was battling with her emotions because she could still remember Liz, but Emma

63

had only been two when Liz was taken and only knew her from photographs.

'You know, girls, I feel like your mum in every way and I love you both as much as if I was, but . . . but I'm not, not really. Liz is your mother and she's been through a terrible time and none of it was her fault. We all have to try to be nice to her.'

'But I don't know her,' Emma said plaintively. 'I can't even remember her. She shouldn't have gone away and left us. She couldn't have cared about us to do that.'

'Of course she cared about us,' Susie said. 'She was pretty and very clever and she was only trying to help people — children.'

'The next few days won't be easy,' Gillian went on. 'Not for any of us. We just have to try our best and make Liz — your mother — feel welcome. Now off to bed, both of you. I'll be along in a little while to say goodnight.'

They went upstairs like lambs, not even bothering with the usual token arguments. Gillian hated to see them both so subdued, but at the same time, she was grateful to them for being so good.

Once they'd gone, she set about tidying up. When she'd finished, she hurried upstairs, but found both girls sound asleep in the bedroom they shared. Susie was curled up in a little ball, the covers wrapped tightly around her. She'd brushed her hair and tied it back in a ponytail. When she was asleep like this, she looked like the child she still was. Any other time, she looked like a young lady in the making, even wearing a little make-up from time to time. That was what she was now, a young lady. She'd been a little girl when Liz last saw her, and Emma had been just a toddler — Emma, who was sprawled across the bed, one foot poking out from under the duvet. No curling up in balls for that one.

Smiling, Gillian tucked her foot back under the covers and it promptly sprang out again. She was a tomboy, a thousand years away from being a young lady; yet it was just around the corner, waiting to happen.

They meant the world to her. She hadn't realised just how much until now. Touching her stomach, unable yet to feel any tell-tale bulge, she knew that the child she was carrying inside her couldn't mean more to her than these two.

The situation was dreadful — bizarre. How on earth would she cope? She looked down at the sleeping girls and knew she had to, some way or other. She simply had to.

How would they sort out their lives? Her head began to spin. What was it going to be like going to bed with David every night knowing that his wife was in the next room? Or would she be relegated to the spare room? Would David ask her to leave?

There would be no easy answers, no straightforward solutions. It was an out-and-out mess, a shambles, and the next few days would be no less than a nightmare.

At first, she'd felt joy that Liz was still

alive and free — joy, elation, happiness
. . . but she'd quickly come down to
earth when she realised what it could
all mean.

She turned to switch off the light.

Liz had been her best friend. They'd
been as close as sisters — closer, even
though they were as different as chalk
and cheese. How on earth was she ever
going to face Liz now?

*　*　*

Following David's directions, Spencer
finally pulled up outside a large house.
Liz saw it at once as the kind of place
David had always dreamed of — old,
rambling, with bags of character and
probably a horrendous mortgage. David,
sitting alone in the back of the car, had
been quiet, deep in thought.

'Will you be all right, Liz?' Spencer
asked. 'I'll call back in an hour or so if
you like.'

'No, that's OK. I'll be fine,' she said,
sounding a lot more confident than she

felt, but she made no attempt to leave the car. 'I'll give you a ring later,' she added, turning to smile at the man who had risked so much to ensure her freedom. 'Thanks, Spencer. You've been great. I couldn't have got through any of this without you.'

She had never been one for sentimental speeches and she wasn't about to start now. There were too many other things on her mind. She looked again at the house, but couldn't bring herself to think of it as being David and Gillian's.

David got out and opened the door for her. They waited until Spencer had driven away, before Liz took the initiative and started up the front path towards the house. Her chest felt sore and tight with emotion, but she knew she had to face this now, or never.

Suddenly, the front door swung open and Gillian was standing there, a girl on either side of her. Liz stopped in her tracks and gasped. How they'd grown.

She'd seen the photographs and David had told her all about them, of course, but it hadn't prepared her for the shock of seeing them in the flesh.

The girls stared at Liz for a moment, then both turned to look at Gillian, as if looking to her to give them a lead. Gently and very nearly unseen by Liz, Gillian gave them both a small push, propelling them forwards.

'Oh, look at you both.' Liz cried at last, her face wreathed in smiles, tears pouring unchecked down her face, tears of joy she wasn't ashamed to shed. 'Aren't you both so pretty. And how tall you are.' She turned to look at David, the happiness on her face enough to send spears of pain shooting through him. Gillian, too, looked away as Liz carried on.

'You've changed, Emma. You look just like me. And Susie, you've grown to look just like your dad. I can't believe it . . . I just can't believe how wonderful you both look. It's so good to see you, like a dream come true.'

The girls shifted uncomfortably, even drawing back a little, embarrassed by

Liz's effusive show of affection.

'Let's go inside,' David said softly and, with his hand resting gently on Liz's back, he shepherded them all into the house.

Liz, trembling from head to toe, moved towards Susie, desperate to hug and kiss her, but the smile Susie gave her was wary and Liz backed off. She turned to Emma, her baby, and held out her arms, but Emma turned abruptly away. Liz was left standing, her arms out and no one to fill them.

All the long, lonely, terrible years had never made her feel so injured and bereft, so utterly alone as she did now. What made it worse, rubbing salt into stinging wounds, was that Emma moved closer to Gillian as if looking to her for protection from this 'stranger'.

'Why don't you sit down, Liz?' Gillian said nervously. 'You look exhausted. I'm glad it's such a nice day for your return. I thought the fog had set in for good. It's been hanging around for ages.' She broke off, aware that she was talking too fast, saying all sorts of inane things. It was the only way she knew to cover her true feelings and hide the emotional turmoil going on inside.

They sat down in the cosy living room, all of them on the edge of their seats, as if it were impossible to relax. Liz didn't recognise any of the furniture. David must have got rid of everything that had belonged to them, as if he'd wanted to wipe her out of his life forever. But that was when he thought she was dead, of course, and now she was here and very much alive.

She looked at the girls. Emma must have been a constant reminder.

'How was your flight?' Gillian asked, breaking the silence. 'We saw the plane land on the news, didn't we, girls?' The girls nodded.

'I don't remember much about it, Gillian, to tell you the truth,' Liz said. 'The last few days have been a complete blur.'

'Haven't you been sleeping? You look so tired.' There was genuine concern and affection in Gillian's voice, but she still looked wary. They all did.

'My sleep patterns are messed up, Gillian. It's going to take ages for me to get back into a proper routine.'

'I'll bet you're just glad to be back,' David said warmly.

'Oh, yes.' Liz sighed. 'I'm so glad to be h . . . '

She'd been going to say home, but this wasn't home. Her home had gone. Before she could sink into a well of self-pity, she remembered the gifts she'd brought for her daughters. 'Oh, I bought you girls something . . . it isn't much, I'm afraid,' she said then to cover her confusion. She delved into her bag. She'd persuaded Spencer to stop on the way here, not wanting to come back empty-handed. The girls wouldn't remember now, of course, but she'd promised to bring them something back when she first went abroad, all those long years ago.

'It's just a perfume spray,' she said, holding out a package to Susie. 'I know you're into all that now from what your dad tells me.'

Susie looked at Gillian for guidance and Liz saw Gillian nod. 'Thank you,' Susie said, taking the package and looking inside. 'Oh, it's my favourite. Thank you.'

'Emma,' Liz turned to the younger girl, 'your dad says you're mad about horses. I got you a book. I . . . I hope it's all right. I would have got something better, but, I just . . . '

Emma stared at Liz, not moving.

'Emma,' Gillian whispered. 'Emma, say thank you, love.'

Emma turned to Gillian and twisted her mouth angrily as if Gillian was betraying her by telling her to speak.

'Go on,' Gillian urged.

'Thank you,' Emma muttered and took the book, giving it no more than a cursory glance before putting it to one side.

If only she knew how much that hurt, Liz thought. It hurt more than any beating she'd had over the past eight years, caused more pain than all the abuse she'd suffered.

No one said anything. Gillian and David were both horrified at Emma's snub, but neither of them knew what to say to ease the situation. It seemed that whatever was said would only make things worse.

The silence dragged on, becoming more and more awkward, until Gillian rose, aware that everyone was looking at her.

'I'll leave you all to talk. There must be so much you want to say. I'll rustle up something for us to eat.'

'I'll give you a hand,' Liz said at once, rising to her feet and following Gillian into the large kitchen.

Gillian's hands shook as she took bowls from the fridge and put them out on the worktop. 'It's just salad,' she said apologetically.

'What can I do to help?' Liz asked.

'Um, you could slice the cucumber.'

'I'd rather not.' Liz smiled. 'I'm not very good with a knife. I seem to have lost all my coordination. Could I wash that lettuce for you?'

'Oh, please.' Gillian nodded.

Liz stood at the sink, looking out over the beautiful garden. This place would be so heavenly, so perfect, if it wasn't for Gillian. Even a simple thing like turning on the taps required concentration and she had to think carefully about which was hot, which cold.

She turned and caught Gillian watching her closely. 'It must have been hell,' she said softly. 'Do you want to talk about it, Liz?'

'I thought I would, but I can't,' Liz replied shakily. 'All I want to do is to forget it and start to rebuild my life. I know that's not very practical, that I'm going to have to face up to what's happened; but right now, I just want to pick up the threads.'

'Oh, Liz,' Gillian suddenly blurted out, guilt making her speak sharply. 'David and I never meant for any of this to happen. We didn't plan it this way. It just happened. You have to understand, we thought you were dead.' She gripped the chair in front of her and stared defiantly at Liz. 'We thought you were dead,' she repeated. 'The government had lost track of you. We'd even been shown a photograph of a body. What else were we to think? We couldn't go on living as we were, in some kind of limbo. It wasn't fair on the children. They needed a proper home, security, love . . . I helped out all I could and, eventually, David and I realised that our feelings for each other went beyond friendship. We needed each other and the children needed us.'

Liz was silent, staring at Gillian. She had some fire in her now. Gillian had always been such a quiet, timid woman, never one for speaking up for herself. And she still wasn't, Liz suspected, not deep down. This outburst would have taken a lot of effort.

The strain was beginning to show. Gillian looked very close to cracking up. 'I'm so sorry, so very sorry, Liz,' she went on. 'But surely you can see how it was, and try to understand? We were friends before. I want us to be friends . . .'

'Friends?' Liz cried. 'You still want us to be friends? You stand there and tell me that you've stolen my husband and my children, turned them against me, and you expect me to understand? You're expecting David's child for heaven's sake! Have you any idea how much of a shock it was when he told me that the life I was coming home to just didn't exist any more? I don't need friends like you, Gillian. You're worse than . . . worse than . . . ' She couldn't bring herself to say it. Couldn't make herself speak of those awful, dark days. 'No, Gillian. We can never be friends, not in a million years. I'm back now, back to stay, and I want my husband and my children back. I'm taking over from here. You'll have to go.'

Gillian stared at Liz in disbelief. She hadn't expected her to accept the situation, but she'd never expected this out-and-out challenge. She put her hands over her face for a moment while she struggled to regain her composure.

Liz was breathing hard. The brief

argument had left her feeling drained, but she sensed victory.

Gillian seemed to stand still for a very long time before, at last, she uncovered her face and looked steadily at Liz, a new determination sparking in her eyes. Her voice was steady and full of conviction as she said, 'Believe me, this was the last thing I wanted to happen, Liz, but it has. David and the girls are the best things that have ever happened to me. I love them more than anything. I'm sorry for all you've been through, I really am, but it doesn't change anything. While there's a breath left in my body, I'll never let them go. Never.'

Liz glared at Gillian. But she knew from the look in her former friend's eyes that she meant every word. She was just as determined to keep David and the girls as Liz was to get them back.

Only one thing was certain now — one of them was destined to be hurt.

3

'Do you have to go out tonight, Mum?' Emma whined. She'd been trailing around behind Gillian all evening, hoping to persuade her to stay home. It was hardly surprising really. Since Liz had arrived the day before, the atmosphere in the house had been almost unbearable.

'You know I do, Em,' Gillian explained gently. 'It's my duty to turn up.'

Any other time she looked forward to, and enjoyed, her regular sessions at the swimming pool with the elderly and disabled group. There was nothing to beat the feeling when one of her pupils swam without armbands for the first time. The looks on their faces when they realised they'd made it after sometimes weeks of hard work was unforgettable.

But tonight, she'd far rather stay home. She didn't want to leave David and Liz alone in the house all evening.

'Why don't you go and watch television, Em?' Gillian suggested at last. 'I have to get ready to go out.'

With a reluctant sigh, Emma went off to the living-room, leaving Gillian to pack her bag. *It's only for a few hours,* she told herself. *What could go wrong in such a short time?*

She had thought of calling in and saying she was ill, but one of her pupils was going to try for a swimming certificate that evening and Gillian knew it was important she was there. Liz's words of the day before kept coming back to haunt her, though.

She wanted David and the girls back and would stop at practically nothing to get them.

Gillian didn't blame her — she'd do the same in her place. She headed towards the living-room and peeped in to check that Emma had settled down and was astounded by what she saw.

She suddenly felt like an outsider, looking in on a happy family scene. They all sat, relaxed, watching a comedy show on TV. Emma was sitting beside David and he had his arm around her; Susie was curled up in an armchair and Liz was in the other armchair, sitting in much the same position.

Frozen, Gillian remained rooted to the spot. They laughed together, made comments about the show, exchanged looks, all of which seemed to bring them closer together. Like a real family. The whole scene made Gillian feel left out, even though she herself had been an integral part of that scene until yesterday. Gillian knew that, if she were to enter the room, the atmosphere would become chilly and conversation would be difficult and stilted.

Maybe it was she who was the problem and not Liz at all.

Moving away from the door, she caught sight of her reflection in the big hall mirror. She looked awful. The strain really was beginning to tell already, in such a short time. Instead of blooming and looking a picture of health as a pregnant woman should, she just looked frazzled.

I'm so frightened, she thought anxiously. *Of losing David . . . the girls . . . the home I've worked so hard to make for the four of us.*

There was so much at stake now. Not only did she love David and the girls, but there was this new baby to think of, too. How could she go out and leave them to their cosy family evening when Liz had apparently managed to slot back into their lives so quickly and easily? What if she came home after the swimming session and everything had changed? What if David decided he wanted her to leave so that he could resume his marriage with Liz? He'd even slept on the sofa last night. He said it wouldn't be right to go to bed with Gillian while Liz was in the next room.

The face in the mirror looked stern. She had to get a hold of herself and stop all this nonsense. David loved her; she mustn't doubt that for a minute.

Picking up her swimming bag, she went back to the living-room, took a deep breath and looked around the door. 'I'm off now then,' she called out cheerfully. 'See you all later.'

They hardly seemed to notice. David raised his hand a little. 'Bye,' he said. 'Mind how you go.'

The girls didn't look away from the television, but just mumbled goodbye while Liz barely spoke at all.

Gillian waited for a second or two, but their attention was firmly on the screen. Liz's sudden laughter triggered giggles from the rest. She was laughing at something on the television, but it hit Gillian like a thunderbolt, and she backed out into the hall, feeling strangely stung and hurt.

At the pool, Gillian tried to put events at home out of her head as she concentrated on her pupils' progress. Lauren was 23 years old and had severe disabilities, but above all she was a fighter. She was a bright, intelligent girl who worked as a legal secretary. She'd been practising hard for her first swimming certificate and Gillian was certain she was ready. 'We'll do it at the end of the lesson,' Gillian promised. 'Margot's going to try for her next stage and Mr Sullivan is going in for his life-saving award.'

The evening passed surprisingly quickly until it was time for the tests. Margot sailed through hers. Mr Sullivan gained his with ease at the grand age of 85, having only learned to swim a year earlier. Gillian was thrilled for them but, when it came to Lauren's turn, nerves got the better of her.

'Come on, Lauren, you can do it.' Gillian urged as the young woman came close to completing a length of the pool.

'I can't,' Lauren gasped, reaching for the side. 'I'm too tired.'

'But you were almost there,' Gillian protested. 'Come on. Try again.'

'Maybe if she had a short rest,' Polly, another instructor, suggested. 'We can hang on for a while.'

Gillian agreed. It was important for Lauren to achieve something tonight after so much hard work and determination. Although she just wanted to get home, she couldn't rush her now at this crucial time. She didn't want the young woman to go home feeling disappointed in herself. So they waited a while until Lauren felt ready to try again.

This time she did it and, when she emerged from the pool, Gillian hugged her ecstatically. 'Congratulations,' she cried. 'I knew you could do it, Lauren. Well done.'

Lauren's husband was waiting outside in his car. It had been worth staying on late just to see the look of joy on his face when Lauren told him her good news. He helped her into the car, then put her wheelchair in the boot.

'Thanks, Gillian,' he said. 'I know she couldn't have done it without you.'

'Of course she could.' Gillian smiled. 'She's a very determined young lady.' But, even as she said it, she knew he had a point. At her first lesson, Lauren had been too frightened even to enter the water and it had taken a long time and a lot of encouragement and reassurance from Gillian to gain her trust.

'Well,' Polly said after they'd driven off, 'it was a very successful evening, wasn't it? Have you time for a coffee?'

Gillian glanced at her watch. She was very late already.

'We could go over the details for the swimming gala,' Polly went on persuasively. 'It won't take long.'

'All right.' Gillian nodded.

Half an hour later, they emerged from the pool building and walked over to Gillian's car. 'I'll give you a lift,' Gillian offered. 'I know you haven't far to walk, but it's very dark.'

'Thanks,' Polly said. 'I don't like walking alone at this time of night.'

'I know.' Gillian smiled. 'That's why I offered.' She pushed her key into the ignition and twisted. Nothing happened.

'What's wrong?' Polly asked.

'I don't know. The engine won't catch. Maybe the battery's a bit flat.'

She tried again and again.

'It's not the battery,' Polly said. 'Your lights are nice and bright. Maybe it's the starter motor.'

'Well, whatever it is,' Gillian sighed, 'it isn't going to go anywhere tonight. I'm sorry about that, Polly. Can I walk home with you and call a cab?'

'Sure, but forget a cab. You'll never get one at this time of night with the pubs chucking out. Why don't you stop over with me? Then you can sort your car out first thing in the morning. I'd appreciate the company with Ken being away at his college reunion.'

How could this happen? Gillian thought miserably. Tonight, of all nights. The last thing she wanted was to leave David and Liz alone in the house, but what choice did she have? Polly was right. She'd never get a taxi now.

Back at Polly's house, she called home. David answered, his voice soft. 'Gillian? Where are you? I was getting worried, love. It's very late.'

'I know, David, and I'm sorry. I can't

get the car to start. I'm calling from Polly's. She says I can stay here for tonight. Her husband's away so she could do with some company.'

'Are you sure you want to stay? I could always drive over to get you.'

'No, it's all right,' she said, secretly hoping he'd argue. 'It's so late, and I know you're still tired from all the travelling. I can't expect you to turn out now.'

'It's probably just as well if I stay here. Liz has gone to sleep on the sofa and I don't want to wake her to keep an eye on the kids. She's very tired too. That's if you're sure.'

Gillian felt numb. She'd wanted him to insist, but he seemed reluctant to leave Liz. A part of her could understand that, but another part strongly resented it. 'I'll see you tomorrow then, David,' she said as brightly as she could.

'Goodnight, darling.'

'Goodnight,' he said softly. 'I love you.'

Back in the living-room, David stood looking down at Liz. She must have been exhausted to have fallen asleep on the sofa. Once the girls were in bed, they'd spent the evening talking and, after her lengthy enforced silence as a hostage, conversation seemed to take it out of her. He still couldn't get over the fact that she was back, and alive, very much alive.

A wave of tenderness washed over him as he began to remember scenes from the time before she was taken away. It had been a wonderful time, a time of passion, and love, and laughter. If she'd crashed out on the sofa in those days, he'd have woken her with a kiss which would ultimately lead to making love.

Without really being aware of what he was doing, he reached out and carefully brushed the hair off her face.

'David . . . ?' Liz opened her eyes slowly, sleepily, looked confusedly around her, then stretched. She'd always reminded him of a cat, even more so now that she was so lean. 'I'm sorry, David, I must have dropped off. Is Gillian back yet?'

'She's not coming back tonight,' he said. 'Trouble with the car. Are you ready for your bed yet, or would you like another drink?' As he spoke, he realised how easily he had dismissed Gillian from the conversation and felt a momentary pang of guilt. But Liz still fascinated him, he realised — perhaps even more so after all this time.

'I'm not tired any more,' she said. 'But don't let me keep you up, David.'

'You're not.' He smiled. 'We've such a lot of catching up to do.' He went to the kitchen and returned with a bottle of wine and two glasses.

'I'm not sure how much of this stuff I can handle now, David.' Liz laughed. She accepted a glass anyway and, as David passed it to her, his fingers brushed against hers and their eyes met. The moment was almost explosive and both held their breath, unsure what to say next.

'You'd just started telling me about your time as a hostage,' he reminded her abruptly. 'Then you fell asleep. Was that a defence mechanism, or do you want to talk about it?'

She was silent for a while, drinking her wine, but her hand was still shaking. Eventually, she took a deep breath and another sip of wine, then began to talk.

'There's not much to say really. I got used to being dirty, feeling hungry . . . being scared all the time and never knowing what was going to happen next. I tried defying them at first, annoying them, you know . . . looking at their faces when I'd been forbidden to do so. I soon learned that wasn't a good idea.'

'They beat you, didn't they?' David asked, his voice cracking as he imagined what she'd been through.

'And worse,' she said, looking away.

He reached out, took the glass from her trembling hand and put it to one side. He put his hand around hers, trying to give her some comfort. 'You don't have to talk about it if you don't want to,' he said softly. In a strange way, he'd never felt closer to her than he did at this moment.

'It seemed that, the more ways they could use and torment me, the more powerful it made them feel . . . Some of the guards were kind and reasonable. Sometimes, months would pass without any ill treatment, but then . . . ' She laughed softly. 'One of the guards brought his little girl in to see me. She was ill. He knew I was a doctor and he wanted me to look at her. It was strange. He was a parent, just like me, worried about his child. It made him seem more human, somehow — for a while.' Her face clouded and she closed her eyes.

'Oh, Liz, I'm so sorry,' David whispered. He felt awful. While he was at home, building up a business, chasing his dreams, falling in love with Gillian, Liz was going through all that. If he'd known . . .

'Has it . . . I mean, all that abuse . . . does it make you feel differently about men? Do you feel uncomfortable with me?' He wanted to comfort, not frighten her.

'Oh, David.' She squeezed his hand. 'I thought it would. I thought I'd never want to have a man even look at me again.' Her eyes searched his, alive and shining. 'But, look.' She gripped his hand, lifted it to her lips and kissed his fingers softly, then held his hand against her cheek. 'No. The answer is no, David, I'm not afraid of you. I love you. I could never be frightened of you.'

He touched her hair, stroked it, and wondered at how soft it was. He realised he was trembling, but whether it was emotion causing it, or the effort it took to hold himself back, he couldn't be sure. His hand slid down her arm, softly stroking. He wanted her so much that everything else was driven out of his mind as he pulled her gently into his arms.

He had to be gentle, careful, slow, so aware that a wrong move could shatter and even destroy her trust in him. It was a huge responsibility, but one he felt able to take on. When he kissed her, he could taste her tears, salty on their lips. He kissed them away. She pushed her fingers through his hair, almost impatiently moving his head so that he was kissing her again on the lips. She accepted his kisses hungrily, passionately returning them.

'Daddy, I can't get to sleep. Can I have a drink?' Emma's voice had the same effect as a bucket of ice-cold water being thrown over them.

David and Liz sprang apart to opposite ends of the sofa, both of them reeling with shock. But David was already coming down to earth with a jolt. What on earth was he doing? Apart from deceiving Gillian, what the hell was he thinking, kissing Liz like that? No matter what she might say, after everything she'd been through, he should not have let things get this far.

He looked at the wine bottle and realised he hadn't drunk that much; not enough to excuse his behaviour by saying the alcohol had taken over. But there was no denying the intensity of his feelings for Liz, and the desire he'd felt. If Emma hadn't come downstairs when she had, there was no doubt what would have happened. Liz had turned his world upside down and awoken feelings he'd long forgotten. So much so, he hadn't given Gillian a second thought. Yet, apart from everything else, she was carrying his child.

Liz jumped to her feet. 'I'll get you a drink, Emma,' she said. 'What would you like? Milk?'

Instinctively, she reached out as she spoke, but Emma shied away.

'I don't want you!' Emma cried. 'Leave me alone. I want my real mummy, not you. Why did you come here? You've ruined everything. I don't like you. Where's Mummy?'

Her outburst finally brought David to his senses. He was on his feet in a moment.

'She's tired, Liz,' he said apologetically. 'She doesn't mean it.'

But Liz was almost overcome at Emma's words. She was Emma's real mum — not Gillian.

As David hurried off to the kitchen with their daughter, Liz sank back into an armchair and buried her face in her hands. Emma had driven it home with brutal force that Gillian meant more to her than Liz. And, even if it were possible to win David back, the girls were going to be another, tougher problem altogether.

* * *

Alone in the house the next morning, Liz did the washing up and clearing away after breakfast. David had gone to work, the girls had left for school, and Gillian was still in town, trying to get her car fixed.

It took Liz twice as long to do anything as it should, and she found she had to concentrate on even the simplest of chores, like washing up. She hated being so slow at everything, but knew it

96

was only a temporary thing. Eventually, she would get back to normal and be able to face the world again on her terms.

Last night, she'd come so close to winning David back. Could he possibly know how nervous she'd felt? How much courage it had taken on her part to let him kiss her? Yet, after the initial fear, she'd relaxed. She couldn't bear to lose him and the girls again, and would do all she could, pay any price, to keep him.

Picking up a packet of breakfast cereal from the table, she took it to the larder, opened the door and stepped back in amazement. The shelves were full, stacked high with all kinds of food. She couldn't believe her eyes. There was so much. Enough there to feed a family for weeks on end. Packet after packet shrieked of added vitamins, extra this, more of that.

For a moment, she remembered that undernourished little girl the guard had brought in to see her. She should have been such a pretty little girl, yet she'd been so thin, her skin ravaged and scarred, her eyes ulcerated, simply because she didn't have enough of the right foods. Liz had always believed, vehemently, that every child in the world, regardless of where they lived, should have the benefit of a proper diet. There was more than enough food to go round, more than enough . . . She put the cereal packet on the shelf and slammed the door shut. There was no reason for anyone to starve or suffer from malnutrition in the world today.

A bell rang and she was puzzled for a moment, trying to think what the noise was. Ah, the doorbell . . .

When she answered the second ring, she found Spencer Ferguson standing on the doorstep, grinning at her.

'Spencer.' She smiled. Her heart gave a strange little flip, but was it any wonder after the way he'd rescued her?

'How's it going?' He grinned. 'Everything all right?'

'Fine.' She nodded. There was no

point in telling him about last night, or about her argument with Gillian for that matter. That part of her life she would have to sort out on her own.

'Could I come in for a minute?'

'Oh, yes, sorry.' She laughed nervously. 'I was just going to make some coffee.'

He followed her through to the kitchen. She didn't blend in here, he thought. This was Gillian's home, not hers. He wondered if she felt as out of place as she looked.

'Can I do that?' he asked, as she filled the kettle and splattered herself with water.

'No, I have to learn.'

It was almost painful to watch her: like a child, determined to get something right, but having to struggle every inch of the way to avoid making silly mistakes. He was shocked that she didn't even have the strength to open the lid of a jar of coffee which had been screwed on a little too tightly.

'I've been approached by some of

your former colleagues,' he said, taking the jar out of her hands and opening it. 'They'd like to have an informal meeting with you if you're up to it.'

'When?'

'Today.'

'What about, do you know?'

'I gather that some of the work you were doing was of vital importance and still is. Your input is still wanted — and needed.'

'Yes.' She sighed. 'I've seen the news programmes, Spencer. The world doesn't get any better when it comes to taking care of children, or people in general. Whenever there's a tragedy, or a war, or a disaster, it's always the children that suffer first. And it's not just abroad, is it? There are children here, at home, who aren't getting a proper nutritious diet. I've been watching some news. I can't believe how many food banks are needed here now.'

'That's the way of the world,' Spencer said.

'It doesn't have to be. In our part of

the world, one of the biggest threats to our health and well-being is malnutrition — not starvation, but eating too much of the wrong foods. I had such a shock this morning when I saw how much food there is in the cupboard, most of it refined and pre-packaged. Cancer and heart disease are endemic in the West, because of our diet. The rest of the world starves while we grow grain to feed animals which then become part of our food chain. Nothing will be gained until we accept we are all part of this world and we all have a responsibility to those sharing it with us.' She broke off and smiled ruefully at Spencer's expression. He looked bemused. 'I'm sorry,' she said. 'It's always been a bit of a hobby horse of mine. When you look at the world as a whole and forget boundaries and racial differences, why should some starve? I just feel very strongly that we have an obligation to others, especially to children.'

'I agree with you,' he said. 'You're preaching to the converted.'

Spencer was even more amazed later, when he accompanied her to the meeting. Despite all she'd been through, she still managed to speak with authority and eloquence. She hadn't forgotten anything she'd learned and, despite only being home for a very short time, she'd brought herself fairly well up to date with the news. When she spoke, her whole being seemed to come alive. His admiration for her grew and grew. Little did she realise it, but she'd already become a huge part of his life, a part of his life he was increasingly reluctant to let go. He'd even surprised himself. Spencer Ferguson knew he had a reputation as a womaniser; he was rarely seen without a beautiful partner in tow. But he'd never felt anything for anyone that even came close to the growing feelings he had for Liz. She was very special.

'Spencer.' He looked up and realised she was looking at him. 'I'm ready to go home now. Thank you for sorting this out and for waiting for me. I don't know what I'd do without you.'

Getting back into the swing of things today had really brought out the best in her, he realised. It took him a moment or two to regain his composure, then he leapt to his feet, waited while she said goodbye to her former colleagues, then held the door open for her as she left the building.

* * *

When Liz left, the meeting broke up, leaving just two senior doctors in the conference room. They stood by the window, watching as Spencer Ferguson led Liz Hargreaves across the car park to his car.

'What did you think, Matthew?' Julian Shaw, the head of the project, asked.

'Of Liz? I'm impressed. I'd heard she was pretty dedicated, but to drive all this way at such short notice and so soon after returning home after her ordeal . . . '

'Well, I had the privilege of working with her before she was kidnapped and I'd say it was typical of her. She's never shied away from a challenge in her life. She thrives on it. But I think much of her strength is in her compassion. She never forgets that we're dealing with *real* people and not statistics.'

Matthew Howard laughed. 'You don't have to convince me, Julian. If you want her back as part of the team, then it's OK with me. She's some catching up to do, but I think she'd be invaluable to us.'

'Did you see how much research material she took with her? She's dedicated, Matthew. She'll put her heart and soul into her work; she always did. I'll get a letter off to her this evening, inviting her to come back. The only problem, if indeed it is a problem, is her over-enthusiasm. She'll fight tooth and nail for what she believes is right and can offend people with her forthright manner.'

Matthew grinned. 'Perhaps if more of us had that kind of courage, the world would be a better place.'

'Oh, I doubt that,' Julian said sadly. 'But still, we have to keep trying, don't we?'

Matthew Howard watched until the car had driven out of the car park and out of sight. 'Who was the man? Someone from the Ministry of Defence?'

'Foreign Office, I believe,' Julian said. 'I suppose they have to keep an eye on her for a while.'

'He was certainly doing that.' Matthew chuckled. 'He hardly took his eyes off her the whole time they were here. Not that I blame him. She's a very attractive woman.'

* * *

'Liz left a note,' Gillian said. 'She doesn't expect to be back until quite late tonight. Apparently, Spencer Ferguson called for her this morning and took her off to a meeting with some of her old colleagues.'

David looked surprised, even a little

put out. Gillian watched him carefully.

'I see,' he said at last. 'Well she didn't waste any time. Did you get the car fixed all right?'

'Eventually.' She pulled a face. 'After many sharp intakes of breath and much shaking of heads. It was the starter motor, but there was a problem with the distributor as well. Anyway, it's running like a dream now.' She was acutely aware that the conversation was forced and even wondered if David being late home from work had any sinister or worrying connotations. Did he have some secret reason for wanting to avoid her, or Liz, or both of them? Everything appeared normal. The girls were in their room, finishing off their homework, David was home, but still Gillian couldn't dispel her feelings of unease. Something felt wrong. The atmosphere in the house had definitely shifted.

'I'm sorry about last night,' she said nervously. 'Was everything all right?'

'Here?' David smiled quickly.

'With you and Liz. Was she OK?'

'Fine, she was fine,' he said. 'She even talked a little bit about when she was a hostage.' He frowned. 'She didn't say much really. It's what she doesn't say that's so telling. We had a couple of drinks, sat up talking until quite late and . . . that was it, really.'

Gillian was relieved to hear that was all. 'It's getting late,' she said. 'I'd better get Emma to bed.'

Upstairs, Susie was sitting at her desk, glaring at her maths book.

'Problems?'

'I don't get it at all, Mum. Why do I have so much trouble with maths?'

'Because you're in such an advanced class for everything else,' Gillian said. 'In a way, you're a victim of your own intelligence. Why don't you take it downstairs, see if Dad can help?'

She gathered her books together, said goodnight to her sister and went downstairs.

'Now, Emma.' Gillian smiled. 'It's time you were asleep.'

'I'm not sleepy,' Emma said. It was strange, Gillian couldn't help thinking. Emma had been growing up so quickly and now she'd reverted to being a 'little' girl again. It was as if Liz's sudden arrival had caused a minor regression. She'd even started taking her old teddy to bed with her again.

Gillian bent down to kiss her goodnight and Emma clasped her hand. 'Will you read some of my book to me?' she asked. 'Please, Mummy?'

'All right.' Gillian smiled. 'What are you reading? Oh, *The Witches*, Roald Dahl. Susie always liked his books.'

She opened the book. 'Just one chapter,' she said and began to read.

★ ★ ★

She became so involved in the story that one chapter became two, then three . . . until she noticed that Emma was almost asleep. Slipping Emma's bookmark between the pages, she closed the book and put it down.

'Goodnight, darling,' she said. 'God bless.'

Emma hugged her teddy tightly and watched Gillian as she tucked her in. 'Mummy . . . '

'Yes, darling?'

'You won't stay away again, will you? I didn't like it last night when you didn't come home.'

'I'm sorry,' Gillian said tenderly. 'The silly old car broke down.' She brushed Emma's hair aside with her fingers and frowned. Emma really was behaving like a little girl. What on earth had happened to bring about this change? She hadn't been like this yesterday. A little clingy, perhaps but . . . 'You weren't worried, were you, sweetie?'

Emma nodded. 'I'm pleased you're back now,' she said sleepily, and yawned. 'I missed you.'

Gillian smiled, but Emma's next words wiped the smile from her face in an instant. 'I didn't like it when Dad was kissing that other lady.'

Gillian gasped, drawing her breath in

sharply. Her head began to spin and she felt sick as the meaning of Emma's words sank in. 'Other lady? You mean your mum?'

'She's not my mum. You are!'

David had been kissing Liz — and Emma had seen them? What else had happened last night? What else had the little girl seen? It was all she could do to suppress her anger and revulsion as she thought of their deceit.

They couldn't wait. She hadn't been out of the house more than few hours and they'd fallen into each other's arms.

She kissed Emma goodnight and walked shakily out of the room, as wave after wave of dizziness washed over her. Outside on the landing, she gripped the banister rail. Shock and anger gave way to sorrow.

How little time it had taken David to deceive her.

4

'Mum!' Emma called from her bedroom. Gillian closed her eyes. She felt as if she was going to be sick. She'd been standing out on the landing, gripping the banister rail for several minutes, listening to David's warm, mellow voice as he helped Susie with her homework downstairs.

David . . . she'd thought he loved her, had placed all her trust in him. Could he really have deceived her so easily, so quickly?

'Mum!' Emma's voice, more insistent, called again from the bedroom. With a conscious effort to mask her pain, Gillian turned and went back into the bedroom where Emma was huddled beneath the covers.

'What is it, love?'

'Will you leave the light on, please? Just for tonight.' She sounded so young, so small and frightened.

'Just until Susie comes to bed then,' Gillian conceded.

'You don't think she's a witch, do you?' Emma whispered fearfully. 'Like in the book?'

It didn't take a genius to work out who she was talking about. Gillian was dismayed to think that Emma should think of Liz, her mother, like that. Whatever else, Liz had always loved her children. She'd been a good wife and mother and, once upon a time, a good friend, too.

'Of course not,' she said. 'She's your mother. She loves you. She'd never do anything to hurt you. There now, settle down and try to get some sleep.' As she leaned over to kiss Emma goodnight, the little girl suddenly flung out her arms, holding tight round Gillian's neck.

'Is she trying to take Daddy away?' she asked urgently. 'I know she's my mother, but . . . but she's a stranger. I don't know her.'

'She'll never take Daddy away from you and Susie, Emma, never. I promise.' Gillian spoke vehemently, from the heart. Again she said goodnight and hurried from the room, leaving the light on this time, and bumped into Susie coming up the stairs, her maths books in her arms.

'All sorted?' Gillian forced a smile.

'Yes, Dad's brilliant.' Susie beamed. 'He explained it all to me.'

'He always was a good teacher,' Gillian remarked softly.

'Night, Mum.' Susie reached up to kiss Gillian's cheek. 'Is the pest asleep yet?'

'Very nearly.' Gillian lowered her voice. 'She's been reading *The Witches* and I think she's got herself a bit spooked. So be nice to her.'

'Aw, silly idiot,' Susie sniffed. 'It's only a story. I suppose she'll want the light on all night now.'

As soon as Susie had gone into the bedroom, Gillian fled to the bathroom, closing the door firmly behind her. All the grief, fury and pain she'd been holding at bay while she dealt with Emma and Susie came flooding over her in a rush.

She stood before the mirror, glaring at her ashen reflection. *How could I let this happen?* she thought desperately. *One night away from home and look what happened.*

Liz had leapt in, taking advantage, and David . . . David, apparently, had welcomed her with open arms. The thought of them kissing . . . And what else had happened? She turned the cold tap on full and splashed her face with the icy water. It chilled her burning cheeks.

What had David said? Something about sitting up late, talking, having a couple of drinks? He'd lied to her — or maybe he'd just been economical with the truth.

Surely he must have known that Emma would say something?

★　★　★

Downstairs, David was reading the evening paper and feeling quite pleased with himself for being able to help Susie with her homework. He sighed and glanced at his watch. Gillian was taking her time settling Emma down to sleep. She'd been upstairs for ages. Maybe she'd fallen asleep while reading the story. He smiled to himself. He'd known that to happen more than once. There would be Gillian, sound asleep, while the girls played quietly, careful not to wake her. She'd be even more likely to drop off now that she was pregnant. He felt a small thrill of delight at the thought of their baby, nestling safe and warm inside.

He was halfway to his feet, having decided to check Gillian and the girls, when the telephone rang. He answered it quickly.

'David . . . ? It's Ted,' a familiar gruff voice on the other end of the line said.

'Ted, what can I do for you?' David asked brightly, although he felt a knot of nervous tension start to form in his chest. Customers calling in the evening usually meant one thing — bad news. Ted Smith was one of his biggest customers. He put regular work David's way and paid his bills on time. If he lost him . . .

'Don't sound so uptight, David,' Ted said, not fooled for a moment by David's false cheerfulness. 'I'm not calling with bad news. On the contrary.'

David released his breath in a long sigh. Not bad news. Thank God for that.

'Germany, Scandinavia and Holland,' Ted went on cryptically. 'They're going overboard at the moment for good British reproduction furniture. Never mind all that pine and plain stuff; they want intricate carvings, plush fabrics. You name it.'

'Just a minute, Ted. You've lost me.'

'It's a hungry market, and growing bigger all the time. So here's my news, David . . . I'm upping my regular order.'

There was a long silence as David

digested the news. He could hear Ted breathing on the other end of the line — waiting, probably with a huge smile on his face, for David's pleased reaction. At last, he managed to croak, 'Upping it?'

'In the long run, it'll be cheaper for me to be able to fill a whole container for export rather than a bit here and a bit there. And once I've got the European market licked, I'm heading west to the States. Do you see what I'm getting at, David? I want more from you, much more. I'm quadrupling my order, and that's just for starters.'

David gripped the receiver. The main part of his business was in restoration, but his real love was in reproduction. Four times as much work would mean he'd have to take on more staff. Roy and Terry couldn't possibly cope with the extra work involved. But more staff also meant buying more equipment and an increased wages bill. And he was up to his limit at the bank. Without the equipment and the extra staff, he didn't have a hope of fulfilling giant orders.

'David?' Ted queried.

Pull yourself together, man, David thought. *Make some reaction. Say something. Anything.*

He blurted, 'That's tremendous news, Ted. Thank you.'

'But?' Ted Smith remarked astutely. 'There is a but, isn't there? You hesitated a little too long just then.'

David smiled briefly. Ted was spot on. He should have known better than to try to fool him. 'I'll have to be straight with you, Ted. I'm not sure I can get together the capital I'll need to fulfil the order.' Even with a quick reckoning, he knew he'd need at least thirty thousand pounds. But where on earth could he get his hands on such a huge sum of money? His bank manager had long since ceased to be sympathetic and he was up to his limit on borrowing. There was an awful silence on the other end of the line. Ted Smith was a good man, warm and friendly, but he was a businessman first and foremost.

'I have to tell you, David, that, unless I can have a firm commitment from you very quickly, I'll have to take the work elsewhere, and that means the existing order, too. I'm sorry to do this to you, but . . . '

'I understand,' David said quickly. 'Can you give me a few weeks to sort something out?' He looked up just then and realised that Liz had come in and was standing in the doorway, watching and listening. He waved his hand at her, indicating that he'd almost finished.

'You're the best and, for that reason, I'm giving you some time,' Ted said. 'I can give you a month — two at most; but after that, I'll have to offer the work elsewhere.'

A month was more than David could ever have hoped for. But, whether he had a month or a year to sort out his finances, he knew in his heart that the situation was probably hopeless.

Liz waited until David had put the phone down before entering the room, a thoughtful expression on her face. He stood up to face her and she saw at once the despair in his eyes. She'd never seen him look so desperately worried. 'Bad news?' she asked sympathetically. 'Is there anything I can do to help?'

Last night, she had felt so close to him, almost as if all the lost years had been swept away. Her heart went out to him now and she longed to be able to do something for him.

'It wasn't bad news,' he said. 'Quite the reverse, on the face of it. A huge new order from one of my best customers.'

'Well, that's wonderful, isn't it?'

'It would be if I had the investment. Look, Liz, I can't take on more work without spending money and, if I turn it down, I blow his small order as well. The point is, I can't afford to lose his small order, because it's regular and it's bread-and-butter work, do you understand?'

'Yes, I understand,' she said slowly.

'What about the bank?'

His short, sharp laugh told her all she needed to know.

'Oh, David.' She moved her hand from where it had been gently resting on his arm and hugged him. 'Something will come up, I'm sure. You'll find a way. I know you will.'

'Thanks, Liz.' He managed a feeble smile and hugged her back. At the very same moment, the door opened and Gillian walked in. Liz felt David's whole body go tense and, when she turned and followed his shocked gaze, she saw Gillian standing in the doorway. She should have felt a thrill of triumph but, when she saw the look on Gillian's face, she felt nothing of the sort.

They all froze, Liz in David's arms, Gillian in the doorway. For a moment Gillian looked shattered, her eyes big and wide in her sheet-white face. Then suddenly her expression hardened and turned as cold as ice, before she spun round and walked out.

'My God,' David whispered and made to follow her, but Liz held on to him, unwilling to relinquish her hold on him.

'Leave her, David,' she said calmly. 'She had to know sooner or later how things stand between us. You can't deny how we still feel for each other?'

David stared down at her, almost as if he didn't know who she was. He shook his head slowly. 'Liz, I don't know right now how I think or feel.'

'Darling, last night . . . '

'Last night, we both had a little too much to drink,' he murmured. 'And you must admit, this whole situation has had us all on an emotional roller-coaster. I still don't know whether I wanted to comfort you or make love to you. Right now, all I feel is confused. We were so happy — Gillian, the girls and I. She's done so much for us.'

'We were happy too, weren't we?' Liz whispered, determined to remind him, but there was real doubt in his eyes.

She felt her legs begin to tremble.

She had to sit down. She had been so sure, last night especially, that she would win David back.

'After you disappeared, Gillian was all that held this family together. I just don't know how I could have coped without her, the girls either. We needed her and she was there for us. And her support wasn't simply emotional, it was financial, too. She put every penny she had into the business, the money her mother left her. She encouraged me to go my own way and give up the teaching job I hated.'

Liz sighed impatiently. 'Money can be repaid. I understand that you feel you owe her something David, but . . . '

'*Owe her something?*' He frowned and nodded. 'I owe her everything, Liz. My life, my sanity . . . Now she's expecting my child and she deserves my loyalty.' He looked at Liz and his tormented expression softened. 'None of this is your fault, Liz. We thought you were dead. Never in my wildest dreams did I ever imagine you'd come back to us. If for one minute I had . . . ' He broke off and shook his head, his eyes filled with sorrow and pain.

Liz knew how much he'd loved her; how much it must have hurt to have lost her. Overcoming his grief and facing up to life without her must have been a terrible ordeal for him, but he'd lived through it.

And now she was back and she still loved him.

'David . . . ' she began.

'I don't know if I can break this family up for you. What am I to do, Liz?' He turned away from her for a moment, trying to conceal the terrible pain in his eyes. 'What am I to do about *you*?' He turned back to face her, his eyes swimming with tears. She could see his heartache etched into every line of strain on his face and she longed to do something to ease his pain.

'The last thing I want is to hurt you, Liz,' he went on. 'What am I to do about Gillian and the baby? And now the business is in danger, too. I've got to think what's best for Emma and Susie, for Gillian and our baby, for you and for the men I employ. I'm being pulled in all directions and I just don't know which way to go.'

'Oh, David, darling . . . ' Liz reached out to him, longing to help him, to hold him and soothe away his pain, but he shrugged her away gently but firmly. 'No, Liz,' he said with a visible effort to regain his composure. 'I'm sorry, but no. This isn't the right time for me to be feeling sorry for myself. I must go up to Gillian and see if she's all right. She's pregnant — she shouldn't have to be suffering like this. This should be the happiest time of her life and between us, we're turning it into some kind of hell for her.'

He rushed out, leaving Liz alone in the living-room. She felt crestfallen, abandoned, but she understood. Yes, of course David must go to Gillian. In her condition, she shouldn't get so upset. But surely once things had settled down, he'd realise that what they had was too good to let go. They were still married, still husband and wife, and the girls made sure they would be bound together forever.

She heard David's feet pounding up the stairs and looked up at the ceiling above her head.

⋆ ⋆ ⋆

David paused for a moment outside the bedroom door, trying to compose himself. Whatever happened, Gillian mustn't see that he was upset. For her sake, he had to appear strong. He pushed open the door and walked in.

Gillian was sitting on the edge the bed, doubled over. She looked up at him, her face deathly pale, her eyes black. He touched her arm and found it cold and clammy. Her hair was damp and sticking to her face, and as he looked at her she moaned softly.

'Gill?'

'Just call an ambulance,' she gasped. 'Quickly, David. It's the baby.'

Spencer leaned on the bar, soaking up the elegant, peaceful atmosphere of the quiet hotel lounge. It was just what he needed right now — soft lights, gentle background music, good wine.

What would have made it perfect, of course, would have been the company of Liz Hargreaves, but she'd insisted on going home.

She'd been marvellous today. Even before he met her, she'd intrigued him and stirred his imagination. Now that he knew her, intrigue had turned to admiration. She hadn't disappointed him.

What a woman. He could listen to her talk all day, but what he really longed to do was kiss her. And if it had been any woman other than Liz Hargreaves, he would have done that by now. But Liz was different; she aroused a completely new set of emotions within him. He took the photograph he'd kept of her from his pocket and looked at it.

His heart turned over. He felt like a kid with a crush.

Hearing footsteps, he pushed the photograph away quickly.

'Spencer, hi. What are you doing here?'

Spencer felt a friendly punch on his shoulder and turned to find himself face to face with an old friend, Steve Gray. For a moment, he forgot all about Liz. 'Steve. I thought you were in Peru.'

'I was until the day before yesterday. This is incredible. Last I heard, you'd gone all respectable on me and had been appointed as a British consul.'

'Nothing respectable about that.' Spencer grinned. 'I just happened to be in the right place at the right time.'

'Ah, a rotten job, but someone had to do it, eh?' Steve laughed, giving Spencer a hefty nudge as he did so. 'I bet it had its compensations though. All those lovely British students lost and alone in a strange country.'

'You must be joking. Drunken sailors missing their ships is more the norm.

It's hardly a tourist trap.'

'You'd have loved Peru. American ladies in distress were my speciality. They could be extremely grateful . . . '

'I can imagine,' Spencer answered drily.

'So, what are you doing now, Spencer?'

'I've finished out there,' Spencer said softly. 'I'm working back here again.'

Steve looked at him for a moment, then said, 'I'll buy you a drink. We've a lot of catching up to do. And you look like a man with a lot on his mind.'

Spencer grinned. Steve had always been the life and soul of the party, even back in their university days. They'd built up quite a reputation as a duo of heartbreakers which had never left them, even though they'd gone their separate ways. Love them and leave them, that was their motto.

'Remember hiding in the shower when that girl was chasing after you?' Steve suddenly reminisced, as if his thoughts had been travelling along the same lines as Spencer's. 'Cute little thing. But, oh, lord, wasn't she persistent?'

Spencer frowned. Yes, he remembered the girl who had big, dark eyes. She'd got a little bit heavy, a little too serious, and so he'd thrown her over. His frown deepened further, though, when he realised he couldn't even remember her name. But wasn't that true also of many of the women in his life? He'd never forget Liz Hargreaves though. Not in a million years.

'Many's the time we'd be seeing one pair of girls down in the lift and rushing to meet another pair coming up the stairs.' Steve laughed.

'They used to queue up outside the apartment building,' Spencer joined in. 'We were quite a team in those days.'

'What do you mean 'in those days'?' Steve guffawed. 'I don't know about you, but I've still got what it takes.'

The barman brought their drinks and Steve downed his at once. Spencer ordered him another, which he dispatched just as quickly as the first.

'Drink up,' Steve urged. 'We'll be late.'

'Late?' Spencer frowned.

'Yeah, I'm going to a party and you're coming with me. It's just your scene — packed to the walls with gorgeous girls.'

'I don't . . . ' Spencer began, but had to smile as Steve interrupted.

'Tall, leggy blondes. Need I say more? It'll be the night of your life, believe me.'

With a lopsided grin, Spencer said, 'Sorry, Steve. Not tonight. You can count me out. I'm afraid you'll have to keep all those gorgeous girls to yourself.'

Steve stared at him open-mouthed for a moment, then he burst out laughing again. 'You've spent too long in the sun, pal. You're kidding me, right?'

'No.'

'Then you're ill. You must be. You've never turned down a good time in your life.'

Spencer downed his drink and turned to grin at his old friend. 'I'm just not interested, Steve,' he said.

'Not interested?' Steve chuckled. 'Next, you'll be telling me you're in love or something.'

As Spencer turned to leave, he remarked, 'Many a true word spoken in jest, Steve. Many a true word.'

He walked out of the bar, aware of Steve watching him. He'd surprised his old friend just now, but he'd surprised himself even more. He'd never turned down the chance to party before in his life.

★ ★ ★

David paced the floor of the hospital waiting room, looking up hopefully every time he heard footsteps approaching. He'd wanted to go with Gillian, but a nurse had taken him firmly by the arm and told him to wait right there, promising to let him know as soon as there was any news.

That had been ages ago. What was going on? He'd held her hand in the ambulance and had been torn apart by the fear in her eyes. She'd looked so vulnerable, and he would have done anything to ease her pain.

For a moment, he stopped pacing and stood at the window, staring out into the black night. He tried to think about Liz, about the business, his daughters, but his thoughts kept returning to Gillian. How tightly she'd held his hand, listening as he'd promised her that everything would be all right. And he'd meant it, every word. For, as much as was in his power, he would make things right.

As they'd rushed her away on a trolley, he'd heard a doctor shouting for a blood match. By then, she was losing consciousness.

It wasn't just the baby. What if he lost Gillian?

'No!' he cried, turning away from the window and looking round the empty, bright room. 'No,' he whispered softly. If anything happened to Gillian now ... He couldn't bear it. He knew that.

She hadn't just been a prop, a shoulder to cry on, a replacement for Liz. Maybe it was true at first, but not any more. Now she was his love, his very life. Without her, his life would have no meaning, no purpose. Without Gillian, he would merely exist. He still loved Liz and there would always be a special place in his heart for her, but he loved Gillian more. Losing Liz had been devastating but, when he thought of losing Gillian, the feeling of loss was ten times worse. The love he shared with her went so much deeper than passion.

'Please, God, don't let it be too late,' he whispered. Too late for him to tell Gillian that she was the one he truly loved; that he wanted her, needed her, more than he'd ever wanted or needed anything or anyone in his life. He thought of Liz — of what she'd already been through, and the effect his decision would have on her. But Liz was strong, a survivor. She'd already proved that. And she had her work. However she might be feeling now, her work had always been, and would always be, of paramount importance to her. Liz was his past, Gillian his future.

'Mr Hargreaves?'

He looked round. He'd been so lost in thought, he'd forgotten to listen for approaching footsteps, and now he found himself facing the same doctor who had taken charge when he'd brought Gillian in. From the expression on the doctor's face, David knew it was going to be bad news. He closed his eyes for a moment.

'I'm so sorry, Mr Hargreaves,' the doctor said as he gently laid his hand on David's shoulder. 'There was nothing we could do. Your wife has lost the baby.'

⋆ ⋆ ⋆

When the taxi drew up and hooted, Liz hurried the girls outside. David had called the night before to break the bad news and to tell her he'd be staying the night at the hospital. Liz had welcomed the chance to be on her own with her daughters, but had been shattered by the dreadful news of Gillian's miscarriage.

It was too soon to tell whether or not there would be any more babies, but the doctors were hopeful. Having had two healthy pregnancies herself, Liz could only imagine what Gillian must be going through. Despite all that had happened, Liz remembered that Gillian had once been her best friend, and her heart ached for her. She'd always loved babies and Liz knew how much she yearned for a family of her own even before all this.

But she also couldn't help thinking that the last obstacle standing in the way of her happiness had now been removed — the baby. It was a terrible thing to think, and she felt ashamed for thinking it, but the thought remained. Nothing stood in her way now, nothing at all. There was no reason for David to stand by Gillian. Yet, he had sounded so shattered when she spoke to him on the phone. He could only be feeling a fraction of the emptiness and pain that Gillian must feel, Liz reckoned, but the loss of his child must be devastating.

'I'll sit in the back,' she told the taxi driver, and slid in beside Emma. 'Soon be there,' she said consolingly to Emma and Susie.

Both girls were white-faced and tense. She'd broken the news this morning after waking them. They hadn't really known how to react. Up till now, the baby had only been real for Gillian and, to a lesser degree, David.

Last night, she'd tried to persuade him to come home to rest, but he'd been adamant. He didn't want to leave Gillian, even for a few hours. She remembered his face as Gillian was carried out to the ambulance. He'd looked so worried, so terrified. You didn't look like that unless you really cared for someone, and cared deeply. Unless you felt guilty and responsible.

Looking at the girls, Liz wished she could have persuaded them to eat breakfast, but none of them had been hungry and she'd ended up scraping the food into the bin. And every time she tried to talk to them, their responses were shy and forced. It was as if they were only comfortable when either David or Gillian was around. *And they're scared*, she told herself. *They're worried and frightened and don't really know what to expect when we get to the hospital.* She did her best to allay their fears, but had the awful feeling that everything she said went in one ear and straight out of the other.

At last, the taxi pulled up outside the hospital and Liz quickly led the girls through the long, clinical corridors, to a small ward at the back of the huge building. After a brief word with the sister in charge, Liz went to the door of the ward and looked in.

Gillian was in a bed next to the window. She was facing away from them, staring out. Beside the bed hung a bag of saline. For a moment, Liz stood with Emma and Susie looking in;

then, suddenly, Emma pushed open the door and rushed in, leading the way. Liz held back, watching the scene as if she played no part. Her feet carried her just inside the ward where she stopped, unable to move another inch. Emma reached the bed as Gillian slowly turned her head.

Her face was white, almost grey, and beneath her eyes were huge dark rings, put there by loss of blood and, of course, grief. But those empty, sad eyes lit up when they saw Emma and Susie. Liz felt a painful jolt as both her girls hugged Gillian, mindful not to disturb the drip. They were laughing and crying, oblivious to her.

This was the kind of reunion she had always imagined for herself. Her lovely daughters running into her arms, weeping with sheer joy at having her home. But it had never happened and would never happen now, she suddenly realised. It had been foolish and unrealistic ever to think it could.

And then, from behind a curtain

where he had been dozing in a chair, David appeared beside the bed, enfolding all three of them in his arms.

A burst of intense physical pain jarred through Liz's body. She reached out and held on to an empty bed. She felt dizzy; the whole room was spinning, and she had to hold on or fall over. Where had he been when she was ill and in pain? Yes, what had happened to Gillian was terrible, but terrible things had happened to her, too, and there was never anyone there to hold her; to whisper sweet, loving words of encouragement and solace. She'd had to face it all alone.

But it was over now. She couldn't change what had happened, just accept it and learn to live with it.

'Are you all right?' The sister had come into the ward and placed her hand gently but firmly on Liz's arm. 'Would you like to come out and sit down?'

'Thank you,' Liz whispered and allowed herself to be led away — away from this family to which she no longer belonged; away from the love she had lost. As she sank down into a chair in the corridor, she knew with all her heart that she was the intruder. Gillian had taken her place, had become the mother of her children, and nothing could ever change that. In her heart, she knew that if she really, truly loved her children, then there was only one thing she could do.

She had to give them up.

The most important thing in the world was their happiness, and the only way she could ensure that was to admit the truth — that David didn't love her any more and that she was an outsider.

'I'll ask one of the nurses to get you a cup of tea,' the sister said kindly. 'Will you be all right here for a moment?'

Liz nodded. She straightened up and took a few deep breaths, struggling to regain control.

She'd thought she knew what it was to feel pain, to ache, to hurt. But it had been nothing to how she felt now.

5

David was about to call out a greeting as he entered his workshop, but something stopped him. Instead, he looked around and felt a surge of pride. The radio was playing quietly in the background as Roy and Terry beavered away, unaware of his presence, totally engrossed in what they were doing. The floor was littered with wood shavings, but the clean, polished tools were hanging in their rightful places on the wall and the benches were clean. Roy was getting to grips with a Windsor chair which had come in with a broken leg. It was a straightforward enough job, but still required a degree of skill and, as the young lad worked, his tongue poked out of the side of his mouth.

Terry, the older man, was busy working on a Tudor-style oak cabinet. The hand carving was almost flawless, but almost was good enough. Absolute perfection was the work only of a machine, and craftsmen were not machines. The piece had been commissioned by a retired army major who had a passion for the Tudor period and had furnished his house accordingly.

It was no use standing here revelling, David thought grimly and turned reluctantly to switch off the radio. The sudden silence made Roy and Terry stop what they were doing and look up.

'Hello, David. I didn't hear you come in. We weren't expecting you in today.' Terry's voice was soft, his eyes full of compassion as he added gently, 'How is Gillian?'

'Weak and upset, but she'll be all right,' David replied. 'Thanks.'

'I sent Roy out earlier to order some flowers from the two of us. I hope you don't mind.'

'Mind?' David smiled. He was deeply touched by their thoughtfulness. 'I think it's a lovely gesture. Thank you.'

'Aw, I know a few flowers won't make

up for what she's lost, but we just wanted her to know we were thinking of her.'

David smiled briefly, then turned to Roy. 'Will you put on the kettle? I want to talk to you, both of you, about work.'

A few minutes later, David sat on a bench. Roy leaned against the wall and Terry sat down on a stool. 'Sounds ominous, David,' Terry said. 'What's the problem?'

'I don't have to tell you how difficult things have been on the work front lately. First the recession is on, then it's off and we don't know whether we're coming or going. The economy's still in a pretty fragile state.' He broke off, slid down from the bench and went to the oak cabinet Terry had been working on. It was an exquisite piece, but had been expensive to make, both in labour costs and materials.

'Apart from the occasional job like this and a few repairs,' he indicated Roy's Windsor chair, 'we've only one regular contract, the one with Ted Smith. It's not much, but it's kept our heads above water. Well . . . ' He took a deep breath and continued, 'I had a call from Ted Smith. You've both met him, and you know what kind of a man he is.'

The men nodded. They waited for David to continue, a mixture of hopeful anticipation and dread on their drawn faces.

'He wants us to take on a new contract producing good-quality repros. It means at least four times as much work, maybe even more.'

'That's great, isn't it?' Roy cried, his face lighting up. As he saw it, more work meant that his job was safe.

Terry wasn't so quick to rejoice, though. He still looked troubled. He met David's gaze steadily and said, 'There's no way we can handle that amount of work, David. We don't have the men or the resources. I hate to be a killjoy, but . . . '

David shot a look at Roy. The young lad was looking decidedly worried now. He hadn't thought of the long-term implications of the new contract, but he was beginning to see what Terry was getting at. 'You're right, Terry. That's just the point. We haven't a chance of meeting that contract. To do it would take even more investment, and we're already up to our necks with the bank. I've been over it a hundred times and there's just no way of getting our hands on the money we need. I've got the house mortgaged to the hilt, so there's no direction left to go.'

Roy walked over and sat on a stool beside Terry. He'd been deep in thought, digesting everything that was being said. 'If we can't take on Ted Smith's new contract, what happens to the old one?' he asked.

'We'd lose it,' David said starkly. 'It's as simple as that. I don't have to spell out for you what that means to a small operation like ours. Without Ted Smith putting regular work our way it's the end of the line for us. It'll be over, just like that. After all we've been through.' He waited for a moment, letting the news sink in. He hated doing this to them. They'd always been loyal, hard-working employees, but their relationship went even deeper than that. They'd stuck together through thick and thin and had become real friends. He couldn't have wished for a better team.

'You don't know how sorry I am to be telling you this,' he said gruffly. 'If there was any way of keeping going . . . You've both been great — the best. I couldn't begin to repay you. And if you want to look for jobs elsewhere, I won't stop you, because I just don't know how much longer I can keep you on. You have to think of yourselves now and, whatever happens, you'll get a shining reference from me.' He put down his cup and turned to go.

'Just a minute,' Terry called out. 'Is that it? Are you giving up just like that, after we've struggled to build this place up?'

David turned back and smiled. 'My hands are tied, Terry. There's nothing I can do.'

'Well, maybe there is,' Terry went on,

casting a sideways look at Roy. 'When my wife's father died, he left her a few thousand. Six thousand and a bit of loose change, to be exact. We've got it put by for a rainy day, you know? She thinks a lot of you, David. She'd be the first to offer it. So, it's yours if you want it.'

'Terry, that's incredibly . . . ' David began, but couldn't continue. He felt too choked. Terry and his wife had been so close to ruin before, that to offer to give him the only money they had was deeply touching and a marvellous gesture.

'Wouldn't it help keep you afloat?' Roy put in eagerly. 'It's a lot of money, and David, I've got an endowment maturing soon. My parents have been paying into it since I was a kid. I was planning to use it for driving lessons and a little car. It's only a couple of thousand, but, well, if it would help, you'd be welcome to it.'

'Thank you, Terry, and you too, Roy. From the bottom of my heart, I thank you both so much. It's . . . it's just so generous and kind, but it's simply not enough. To keep going, we'd need an investment of at least £30,000. If . . . when the time comes for us to close, you're going to need that money as a cushion. I couldn't take it from you just to keep going for another month or so. It'd just be throwing good money after bad.'

Terry nodded sadly. 'I guess so,' he said. 'But I had to try. You can't blame me for that.'

The three men stood for a moment, deep in thought, as the implications of what had happened slowly sank in.

'You've been a great boss, David,' Terry said at last. 'You gave me a chance when I'd lost all hope of ever working again. You gave me back my self-respect and made me feel worth something again. I'm going to miss you as much as the work.'

'That goes for me, too,' Roy said. 'You've been great, more like a friend than a boss. And you've given me a start, which is more than I got anywhere else.'

David, with some difficulty, swallowed the lump which had formed in his throat. He was so moved, so touched. He'd just told these two men that he was going to be making them redundant, and they were thanking him. 'I couldn't have done any of this without you,' he went on. 'Thank you, both of you, from the bottom of my heart. But the truth is that we've about seven or eight weeks' work left, and after that . . . ' He shrugged his wide shoulders and let them fall in a gesture of defeat. 'Who knows?'

⋆　⋆　⋆

Liz had chosen her moment carefully, waiting until she knew David would be at work and the girls at school before calling a taxi to take her to the hospital. Once there, she made her way quickly to the ward. Gillian was off the drip now, but still looked weak and drained. Liz hesitated for a moment before entering, but she'd made up her mind and she'd never been one for backing down once a decision had been made.

Gillian was sitting up, propped against pillows. A number of books and magazines were scattered on her bed, but she'd obviously made no attempt to read them. The fruit in the bowl on her locker and the chocolates she'd been given remained untouched.

'Gill.'

She turned at the sound of Liz's voice and immediately a veil seemed to drop over her eyes. She looked wary, guarded and tense. *Is she so afraid of me?* Liz wondered.

'Oh, I nearly forgot. I got you these. You always liked them.' Liz held out a small bunch of freesias and felt a pang when Gillian's eyes momentarily softened as she took the flowers. She smelled them and smiled. 'They're lovely. Fancy you remembering.' She seemed genuinely touched, and Liz was glad she'd made the effort to find freesias. It would have been easy to grab the first bunch

151

of flowers she found, but deep down she wanted to please Gillian, to make her happy.

Then, for a moment, Gillian stopped smiling and her face creased with pain. It was nothing physical, but a pain Liz could understand only too well. 'We were such close friends in those days. It's hard to believe how it could all go so wrong . . . '

With a rueful smile, Liz sat down on the chair beside the bed, then said philosophically, 'Nothing lasts forever, good or bad.'

The guarded look was suddenly back in Gillian's eyes.

A healthcare assistant came over with a small vase for the freesias and placed them on the trolley. 'Aren't they pretty?' she remarked with a cheerful smile. 'They have such a lovely smell, don't they?' With that, she turned around and bustled away.

'Why are you here, Liz?' Gillian asked then.

'I have to talk to you. Firstly, to say

how very sorry I am about the baby.'

Gillian turned her face to one side, burying it in the pillow for a few seconds. She was still so raw, Liz thought.

'I didn't come here to hurt you, Gillian,' Liz continued tenderly. 'Whatever has happened, I do still care about you, you know. I haven't forgotten that we were once good friends. I suppose what I'm trying to say is, we're all victims in this. You and David and the girls didn't mean to hurt me and I never dreamt of the hurt I'd cause by coming back. All I ever wanted, all I hoped and prayed for, was to have my husband and family back and to lead a normal life again.'

At this, Gillian seemed to find some inner resource of strength. She struggled to sit up so that she could meet Liz's gaze. 'I still grieve for the baby and I don't feel too good, but I'm as determined as ever to fight for David and the children and the baby we may still be able to have one day. Who knows? The doctors say there's no reason why I shouldn't conceive again.'

Liz smiled gently, feeling a surge of affection for her friend. 'Relax. I haven't come here to fight with you. I'm not that awful, surely? The time for fighting is past, over with. Yesterday, I saw you and David and the girls and I suddenly realised how right you all look together. It wasn't just that either. I realised you were right, the four of you. You belong together and I . . . I just don't belong any more. So I've come to say goodbye.' The last was said with just a small lapse into hesitation which Liz quickly corrected. This was no time to lose heart, to doubt that what she was doing was the right thing. For to stay, to fight, would mean destroying the happiness of those people she loved most in all the world, and she had no right to do that.

Gillian was staring at her, shocked. At last she said, 'Liz, whatever do you mean?'

'Cruel fate took your baby away from

you, Gillian, and I'm sorry for that, but you had no choice in the matter. Me, I'm having to walk away from my children and the man I love, and I'm doing it from choice. It wasn't an easy decision to make. All those years in captivity, it was simply the thought of them waiting at home for me that kept me alive. And now I'm walking away from them. Have you any idea how that feels?'

Gillian, for a moment, tried to put herself in Liz's shoes. So far, she'd seen her only as threat to her happiness and security, blocking out the awful things Liz must have suffered. But it was there, etched forever in her face. She had no idea how it felt to have to turn your back on those you loved, but she could imagine it only too well. Having just lost her own child — to know that kind of pain — she could really feel for Liz at last and appreciate the sacrifice she was making.

'Is there any chance . . . ?' Liz began. 'I mean, we've known each other such a long time. Do you think we could be friends again?'

Gillian's heart leapt. She'd missed Liz, too, her friendship and company. Although they had little in common, they'd always got along well. 'We were friends a long time,' she murmured and, before she could stop herself, her thoughts began to travel back through time to happier moments. 'Liz, do you remember when we went on the working holiday in France? And the guy with black, bushy eyebrows who had a crush on you?'

'Maurice? Yes.' Liz smiled. 'He was rather sweet, but not my type, I'm afraid.'

'You couldn't go anywhere without tripping over him,' Gillian recalled, laughing.

'You should talk. There was that young fellow who kept leaving little notes under your windscreen wipers.'

'My mystery man.' Gillian giggled.

For a moment or two, it was as if the past few years hadn't happened, but then Gillian became serious again. 'You will still keep in touch though, won't you? For your sake, as well as David's and the children's? It's still early days for Emma and Susie, but you are their mother, nothing can ever change that. I know that you will be close to them again; they just need a little more time.'

Liz simply nodded.

'What are you going to do, Liz?'

'I'm going to do what I've always done best,' Liz replied stoically. 'I'm going to work, to do my best for other children less fortunate than my own. Things have changed while I've been away. Children here need my help. Did you know there's been a resurgence of poverty-related illness? I certainly didn't. I can't do anything to relieve poverty, but perhaps I can help educate people so that whatever food they do eat is at least doing them some good. I know I go on about it a bit, but I feel so strongly about this. Nobody should suffer, especially not children.'

Gillian's eyes shone with admiration. This was the Liz she had always known and loved. Fiercely determined to help anyone worse off than herself, at whatever cost. 'Good luck to you, Liz,' she said vehemently. 'I mean it. I wish you every happiness in the future. God knows, no one deserves it more than you.'

'Thanks,' Liz said. 'Tell David . . . tell him I won't stand in his way if he wants a divorce . . . ' Her voice almost broke. 'Divorce' was such an ugly word, and to use it with regard to David and herself was heart-breaking. She quickly pulled herself together, though, and forced a smile.

Eyes brimming with tears, Gillian reached out and took Liz's cold hand in her own. 'Thank you,' she whispered, meaning it from the bottom of her heart.

'I . . . I should go,' Liz said, getting to her feet. 'Sister keeps glaring at me. You're meant to be resting. Goodbye, Gillian.' She smiled wanly, then turned and walked away, each footstep carefully measured. As the distance between her and Gillian became greater, so her steps became faster, firmer, and her back straighter.

Outwardly, she looked every inch a confident, self-assured woman with everything to live for. It was a lie. Inside, she felt a savage loneliness like nothing she'd ever felt before, not even in her years of captivity.

★   ★   ★

It was possibly the worst of locations — an old, disused warehouse in a run-down inner-city area, where the paint peeled from the walls and broken windows had simply been boarded up, while the remaining windows were sooty from city grime.

Yet it was full of noise: children laughing and shouting, while their parents also had to shout to make themselves heard above the all-pervading din. Most important of all, the food was vanishing rapidly — a sure sign that it was being enjoyed.

Since she'd been put in charge of this

project, Liz had seen tremendous results. In the past three weeks, there was an improvement right across the board, from the attitudes of the children to healthy eating, to the involvement of parents and grandparents in the scheme. And what wonderful characters she'd met, particularly among the children. The mischievous scamps were just as deserving of the best life had to offer as any other child.

She smiled and thought suddenly of Spencer. She wouldn't mind betting he'd been a bit of a scamp when he was a child. There was so much she had to thank him for. Without his efforts, she had no doubt she would still be languishing in that foreign hell — or dead. But his involvement hadn't ended there. He'd taken charge, taken her under his wing, helped her to get started again. Saying goodbye to him had been so touching. She'd never forget the look on his ruggedly handsome face as he tried, clumsily, to tell her how fond he'd become of her.

'As long as I live, I know I'll never

meet another woman like you, Liz,' he'd said. 'And I will always admire and respect you.' His look had become wistful and Liz had felt a strange little shiver run down her spine.

'So, what are you going to do with all the money that's coming to you?' he'd asked suddenly, changing the subject abruptly. 'It must run into tens of thousands. You're a rich woman, Liz. You could retire and spend the rest of your life with your feet up, living the life of a lady of leisure.'

Putting her feet up. Being a lady of leisure. The very thought made Liz laugh out loud. Spencer had grinned, too. He knew her better than that. But she didn't want a penny of the money, not for herself.

'I've got very definite plans for that money, Spencer,' she'd said, and then she'd reached up to kiss his cheek, noticing a strange look in his eyes — an odd expression she found impossible to decipher. If she didn't know better, she'd have said it was longing, but that was quite impossible of course. They lived in different worlds. A guy like him could have any woman he wanted, and his interest in her had been purely the challenge of gaining her freedom.

'Penny for them, Liz?'

She jumped at the sound of a familiar, deep male voice behind her and felt colour flood into her face.

'You startled me.' She laughed.

He grinned. 'Sorry, didn't mean to.'

Dr Andrew Jarvis was a local G.P. who was also very much involved in the programme. He had dark, wavy hair and vivid blue eyes and was extremely attractive in a classic, square-jawed way. What Liz liked most about him was his dedication, although she wasn't oblivious to his quite substantial charm either, a charm he had used to its full advantage since her arrival. He'd welcomed her into the fold and made her feel very much a part of things right from the start.

'Will a penny cover the cost?' he asked.

'Oh, I should think so.' She smiled. 'I was just thinking how much happier these kids are already. You should be seeing a lot less of these nutritional disorders in your surgery within a few weeks.'

'I already have,' he said. 'You've worked wonders here, Liz. I know this programme is going to be a great success, but there's plenty more to be done and we have a fight on our hands when it comes to funding.'

'I'm good at fighting,' Liz remarked drily. 'Anyway, I can't take the credit for all this. I couldn't have set it up without your support, nor could I keep it going without you.'

He was clearly pleased and managed a modest smile before asking, 'Doesn't all this food make you hungry? We need our sustenance, as well you know. Would you like to go out for a meal tonight?'

'Tonight?' She smiled enigmatically. 'I'm sorry, I can't tonight. I've already made arrangements. Some other time, perhaps?'

'I'll look forward to it,' he said.

She looked away before he saw the lie in her eyes. She just wasn't ready yet.

But she had to move on sooner or later.

'Wait,' she said. 'If the offer's still open, I'd love to.'

* * *

Spencer took off his hard hat and ran his fingers through his hair, ruffling life back into it. He looked down at his mud-caked boots and then around the busy site. This was a far cry from his last job. There, his worst problem had been the arid heat. Here, the problem was too much water, with pumps going day and night to keep the site dry.

He noticed a four-wheel drive drawing up, bumping over the rough tracks and coming to a halt beside him.

'Hey, Spencer, I thought I'd find you here.' The driver leaned out, grinning all over his face.

Spencer laughed when he saw Steve Gray behind the wheel. 'Hi, Steve,' he said. 'What brings you out here? I thought building dams was your bag these days.'

'So it is. I haven't come to admire your handiwork, but to invite you to a party — my leaving party, to be exact. I'm going back to Peru on Friday.'

'Sure,' Spencer said. 'Just tell me where and when and I'll be there.'

'Hallelujah! Tonight, around ten-thirty, at the Rosy Flamingo.'

'The rosy what?' Spencer guffawed.

'Hey, it's a classy place, Spencer. Nothing but the best for the best. And don't worry about bringing a partner; it's all arranged. I've asked all the old crowd along, so it's going to be great do.'

'What's this about a partner?' Spencer asked warily.

Steve tapped the side of his nose. 'You won't be disappointed. This girl has everything! The face, the figure, the lot.'

★ ★ ★

Later, when Spencer had showered and laid out the clothes he was going to wear, he poured himself a drink and carried it through to his bedroom. Sitting down on the bed to put on his watch, his eyes strayed to the picture of Liz on his bedside cabinet. Her smile brought back a multitude of memories. He remembered the first time he'd seen her, how thin and bedraggled she'd looked, nothing at all like the beautiful woman in his photograph. But even then, with her hair dirty and her cheeks hollow, he'd felt something for her. How he'd longed to pick her up in his arms and hold her until all her pain had gone.

Then there was her rescue and her dependence upon him. For a while, he'd been completely responsible for her. The urge to look after her, shield her, protect her, had been overpowering. Yet how quickly she had recovered, and now she was simply gorgeous again. When he thought of all the beautiful women he had known, they faded in comparison to Liz, for she had a rare inner beauty as well.

He turned to look at his dark suit waiting on the bed. He knew he looked good in it and he'd have no trouble attracting female company, whether Steve had fixed him up or not. But it all seemed so hollow and meaningless when there was really only one woman he wanted to be with.

A few moments later, he was dialling the number of the Rosy Flamingo and speaking to the manager. 'Would you pass a message to Steve Gray for me, please? Tell him . . . tell him Spencer Ferguson won't be able to make it tonight after all.'

When he'd hung up, he went back to the lounge and poured himself another drink. He'd fancied himself in love many times before, but he'd never known it to hurt like this.

* * *

Gillian squirted a generous dash of maple syrup on the pancake and handed it to Emma. 'That's the last one,' she said. 'If you want any more, you'll have to make them yourselves.'

'Pancakes for breakfast.' David grinned. 'You spoil them.'

'I didn't see you turning them down,' Gillian reminded him. 'In fact, you probably ate twice as many as everyone else.'

'Guilty,' he said, putting up his hands. 'As my waistband will no doubt testify.'

David couldn't believe how good he felt, in spite of everything. For, today, the first thing he'd have to do was call Ted Smith, to tell him he'd been unable to raise the finances. He'd tried and failed, and it wasn't fair to keep Ted dangling any longer. He owed it to him to come clean. He'd have to wave goodbye to his business and tell Roy and Terry that it was finally over. But somehow it just didn't seem so important anymore. As he watched Gillian laughing and talking with the girls, the loss of his business just faded into insignificance when he thought how close he had come to losing her.

She caught his look and smiled, and he felt his heart turn over. Impossible as it seemed, he loved her more than ever. It was as if Liz, by coming back into their lives and then leaving again, had exorcised something within him, releasing him once and for all.

'Postman!' Susie yelled suddenly. 'I'll get it.'

'My turn!' Emma bleated.

They both charged out of the kitchen, and for a quiet moment Gillian and David exchanged looks. She knew how important today was going to be for him, but like him, she was resigned to it. The worst had already happened and whatever came next, they still had each other.

'Hold it! Hold it!' David cried as his daughters rushed back from the front door. Susie was holding a letter out of her sister's reach and Emma was leaping up and down trying to grab it.

'Thank you,' he said, pretending to be cross as he took the letter. 'It's addressed to you, Gillian. It's from Liz.'

Gillian tore it open, aware that everyone else was watching. Why had Liz written to her? But . . . why not? They were friends, weren't they?

Inside the envelope with her letter were three more envelopes, one for each of the girls and one for David. Emma and Susie took their letters and began to open them, reading quietly to themselves.

'What does she say?' David said. 'It looks like a long letter.' He seemed reluctant to open his. Gillian's eyes scanned the three neatly written pages, picking out key words here and there. She'd take time to read it properly later, when she was alone. Now, she outlined it to David.

'The project's going well, and she's settled into her apartment. It's mainly about the kids she's working with. She sounds as if she's really fond of some of them. And, oh . . . '

'Oh?' David echoed.

'That G.P. she mentioned in her previous letter, Andrew Jarvis. Apparently she's been out to dinner with him.'

David's face broke into a grin and Gillian knew his pleasure at this news was genuine. All he wanted for Liz now was to see her happy and settled.

'Oh, here . . . she says that Spencer Ferguson has been in touch. Reading between the lines, I'd say she's quite pleased. She hadn't heard from him for a while, then he called her out of the blue. All in all, it sounds as if she's doing all right,' Gillian murmured.

David reached across the table and touched her hand. 'So are we,' he said, feeling another rush of warmth and love for Gillian.

'What about yours?' she asked him.

He remembered his own letter then and tore open the envelope. Gillian watched nervously. Inside, he found a cheque and a note, on which were written just two words, 'Happy Recovery'.

Suddenly, David flew back in time to when he and Liz had first married. The first thing they had ever bought for their new home was an old armchair. It was a beautiful, solid piece of furniture, but in desperate need of re-upholstering. David had worked on it in the evenings, at weekends, and every spare moment. Creeping in to see how he was getting along, maybe bringing him a cup of coffee and some sandwiches, Liz would always creep out again, calling over her shoulder, 'Happy recovery.' It was where his passion for antiques and restoration had begun, and the two words had become their catchphrase. No one else understood what it meant, and that made it all the more special.

Now, those words meant something entirely different. They were all on their way to recovery in one way or another. Shaking himself from the memories the words had rekindled, he looked properly at the cheque for the first time. He thought he was seeing things and shook his head.

But it was real — and it was right there in front of him. He could hardly believe his eyes. He stared at the cheque again until his vision blurred and his hand began to shake.

'What is it?' Gillian asked, rising to her feet.

'Daddy, is everything OK?'

'OK?' David echoed, coming to his senses, also getting to his feet. 'Everything's more than OK. Everything's wonderful. And that's just the beginning. From now on, it can only get better.' Emma was still staring up at him as he grabbed hold of her and swung her round.

'David?' Gillian looked anxious and bemused, happy that he was happy, but also a little scared. He pointed to the cheque on the table. Gillian looked at it, her eyes widening in disbelief. 'Thirty thousand pounds. Oh, David!' she cried, rushing into his arms. He gathered all three of them together in a giant hug and danced them all around the kitchen. Life had never been better.

'We'll pay her back,' he said. 'Once we're in profit — and that shouldn't take long — we'll pay her back.'

Gillian was still scanning her letter. 'She says you're to keep it,' she said incredulously. 'That you and the girls suffered as much as she did and she wanted to share the money with you to help secure their future.'

'Let's invite her over to stay sometime, Dad,' Susie said. 'We'd like to spend some time with her.'

They all looked at Emma and she nodded, her eyes brimming with tears. 'She's still our mum,' she said, then she smiled. 'We're lucky to have two lovely mums.'

* * *

Liz looked across the table at Spencer, a smile on her lips. They'd just finished a wonderful meal and she felt as if she were glowing. She'd been out a couple of times with Andrew, but although they got on well, the chemistry just wasn't there. She'd thought it was just her, until Spencer had called — and now she realised it wasn't her at all.

'What are you thinking?' he asked.

'Oh, that you look a lot different tonight than you did when you rescued me.'

He laughed. 'Well I was dusty, dishevelled — I'd just travelled across a desert to get to you.'

Her smile faded and a serious expression took its place. 'I know you had, Spencer. I never realised at the time. I was so numb, and it all felt unreal, but do I remember correctly that you pushed that gun away and told the guy he wouldn't need it? Did you really do that, Spencer?'

'I might have done.' He grinned. 'I've never liked people pointing things at me, whether it's fingers or guns or anything else.'

'You could have been killed for that.'

'You were worth the risk,' he said, and his eyes met hers across the table. The band began to play and he stood up. 'May I?' he said, holding out his hand.

She reached up and her whole body

tingled as he took her hand in his and led her to the dance floor, pulling her gently into his arms. She rested her head against his shoulder as they moved to the music. She recalled how safe she had felt when he'd held her before, all that time ago. For a long time he'd been part of it, part of the world she'd wanted to leave behind. But she was beginning to see him as something else: her saviour. The guy who had risked everything to rescue her when he didn't know her from Adam.

When the music stopped, they paused on the dance floor, unwilling to return to their seats. She realised that from the very first moment, she'd felt safe in his arms. Always. But not just that. She was feeling something else now, something exciting.

'Thank you for agreeing to come out with me,' he murmured huskily against her ear. 'I thought you had a real thing going with that doctor and that I had no chance.'

'Thank you for asking me,' she

replied, looking up at him. His mouth was so close to hers. Seconds away. Their lips met and her whole body tingled again as she tightened her arms around his neck.

Life was about to get even better, and she finally felt that she'd come home.

THE END

We do hope that you have enjoyed reading this large print book.

Did you know that all of our titles are available for purchase?

We publish a wide range of high quality large print books including:
Romances, Mysteries, Classics
General Fiction
Non Fiction and Westerns

Special interest titles available in large print are:
The Little Oxford Dictionary
Music Book, Song Book
Hymn Book, Service Book

Also available from us courtesy of Oxford University Press:
Young Readers' Dictionary
(large print edition)
Young Readers' Thesaurus
(large print edition)

For further information or a free brochure, please contact us at:
Ulverscroft Large Print Books Ltd.,
The Green, Bradgate Road, Anstey,
Leicester, LE7 7FU, England.
Tel: (00 44) **0116 236 4325**
Fax: (00 44) **0116 234 0205**